THREAD
AND GONE

Lea Wait

KENSINGTON PUBLISHING CORP.

http://www.kensingtonbooks.com

KENSINGTON BOOKS are published by

Kensington Publishing Corp.
119 West 40th Street
New York, NY 10018

ISBN-13: 978-1-61773-008-5
ISBN-10: 1-61773-008-4
First Kensington Mass Market Edition: January 2016

eISBN-13: 978-1-61773-009-2
eISBN-10: 1-61773-009-2
First Kensington Electronic Edition: January 2016

10 9 8 7 6 5 4 3 2 1

Printed in the United States of America

Chapter 1

*The world, my dear Mary, is full of deceit
And friendships a jewell we seldome can meet
How strange does it seem that in searching
   around
The source of content is so rare to be found.*

—Poem stitched by thirteen-year-old
   Lucy Ripley,
   Hartford, Connecticut, 1802

The simple folded leather packet looked old. Old, cracked, and very out of place, as it lay innocently on the bright red Fourth of July tablecloth. A mystery from the past had interrupted my first Haven Harbor dinner party.

Before I'd seen that packet and its contents I'd been feeling high on more than the Pouilly-Fuissé recommended by the owner of Haven Harbor's local wine and gourmet treats store.

(Buying beer? No problem. Wine? That's a whole different world.)

I'd gotten up the courage to invite Sarah Byrne, Dave Percy, and Ruth Hopkins, the three other Mainely Needlepointers who were going to be alone on the holiday, to join me to celebrate the official start of the tourist season, and my first Maine Fourth of July in ten years. (Ob Winslow and Katie Titicomb were celebrating with family.) I figured all three of my guests would be understanding if my salmon was a little dry or my peas undercooked.

But until the packet arrived, everything had been perfect.

I'd pulled it off. My guests had made appropriate compliments and serious dents in the baked salmon, fresh green peas, and hot potato salad that made up my close-to-traditional New England Fourth of July menu. And I'd only had to interrupt Gram's Quebec honeymoon twice to ask for cooking advice and counsel.

As I looked around the table I couldn't help smiling. Two months ago I hadn't known these people. Today I counted them friends as well as colleagues.

Gram had brought us together. She'd gathered an eclectic and talented group of Mainers to do custom needlepoint for her business, and as the new director of Mainely Needlepoint I was reaping the benefits of her choices. Not only could everyone in the business do needlepoint, but they'd all brought their own personalities and talents to their work.

Anyone meeting us for the first time would

never guess that middle-aged Dave, navy retiree and now high school biology teacher, also had an extensive garden of poisonous plants. Or that Sarah, whose pink-and-blue-striped white hair and Aussie accent made her noticeable in a small Maine town, was also a member of the staid Maine Antiques Dealers Association. Or that Ruth Hopkins, a sweet little old lady whose arthritis forced her to depend on her pink wheeling walker, wrote erotica.

And me, Angie Curtis. The most ordinary of the lot. As long as you understood that "ordinary" included ten years working for a private investigator in Arizona. I knew how to use the gun I now kept hidden under Gram's winter gloves and scarves in the front hall. I was also the youngest of the group—twenty-seven—a born Mainer, and a native of Haven Harbor. Most unusual in this crowd, I was just beginning to learn needlepoint.

I was also learning what it was like to live alone. Gram's wedding to Reverend Tom last weekend had been pronounced "a smashing success" by Sarah, and as soon as Gram returned from her honeymoon, she'd be moving to the rectory. True, I'd lived alone (nearly all of the time, anyway) in my Arizona apartment, but being alone in two rooms was different from being alone in a large creaking house built over two hundred years ago.

But I'd grown up here, as my mother and grandmother and great-grandmother had before me. I couldn't imagine another family in these rooms. I'd get used to living here by myself. In the meantime, my only full-time companion was Juno, Gram's large Maine coon cat.

Juno looked up expectantly when anyone came into the house and then curled up in Gram's favorite chair, sadly waiting. She didn't understand about honeymoons. To make up for Gram's absence, I'd been giving Juno more treats than I'm sure Gram would have approved.

I'd even slipped a piece of salmon into her dinner dish before I served my guests. And I suspected Dave had been passing her a few tidbits under the table during dinner.

The four of us had comfortably finished off two bottles of wine and were debating the virtues of strawberry-rhubarb pie now, or strawberry-rhubarb pie after the fireworks, when we heard a knock on the front door.

The young people standing there could have been any two Haven Harbor teenagers celebrating the Fourth.

But they weren't.

Chapter 2

When gold and silver threads are used for Embroidery they are generally associated with coloured silks and filoselles [soft silk threads]. When used for Ecclesiastical purposes the work is called Church Work. The same kind of work is occasionally also used for secular purposes.

—Sophia Frances Anne Caulfeild and
  Blanche C. Saward, *The Dictionary of Needlework: An Encyclopedia of Artistic, Plain and Fancy Needlework*, London, 1882

The stocky young man standing on my front porch had his arm firmly around the girl's waist. I couldn't miss his red, white, and blue tank top emblazoned with New Hampshire's "Live Free or Die" motto or the purple anchor tattooed on his left shoulder.

The girl looked even younger than he was—slight, with wispy blond hair that covered part of her face.

I didn't recognize them.

"Sorry to bother you," said the young man. "Angie Curtis?"

"Yes?" I answered. The silence in back of me said my guests were listening. Living in a small town offered little privacy. If you forgot what you'd done yesterday, you could always ask your neighbors. Deep secrets, on the other hand, might be hidden for years, especially from outsiders.

"My brother, Ethan, said you might be able to help us."

For a moment I didn't connect. "Ethan?"

"Ethan Trask. He said you knew each other in high school."

Blurred images flashed through my mind. Handsome Ethan, the boy I'd had a serious crush on in junior high school. Ethan and his friends, teasing the younger girl who'd followed him around. And, more recently, still handsome Ethan Trask, the Maine state trooper and homicide detective who'd helped me discover what happened to Mama years ago. The Ethan whose wife was serving in Afghanistan, leaving him unavailable, and a devoted single parent.

"I know Ethan. You're . . ."

"His younger brother. Rob." He stuck his hand out to shake mine. His skin was rough; the skin of someone who worked outside, most likely in construction, or, based on his anchor tattoo, on the sea. "I'm eleven years younger than Ethan. You probably don't remember me."

"No, sorry. I don't." I did the math quickly. Rob must be about twenty-one. He would have been eleven when I'd left Haven Harbor to head west. No wonder I didn't remember him.

"And this is Mary," Rob said, pushing the young woman next to him toward me. She brushed her hair off her face and smiled shyly. "Mary Clough. My fiancée."

"Nice to meet you both," I said. Clough. The name was familiar, but I couldn't place it. I remembered a lot about growing up in Haven Harbor, but in those years I'd been focused on my own problems, and on my high school classmates, not on other families in town. Mary would have gone to Haven Harbor Elementary then. She looked barely sixteen. Probably still in high school.

Some Mainers married young. And divorced young.

Behind me, my guests were migrating from the dining room to the front hall. I turned to acknowledge them. "These are my friends, Sarah Byrne, Ruth Hopkins, and Dave Percy. Maybe you know Dave. He teaches biology at the high school."

Rob shrugged. "I didn't take biology."

Mary nodded slightly. "I know Mr. Percy." She hesitated. "We're sorry to interrupt your party. But Ethan and Mrs. Trask said you might be able to help me." She reached into a small plastic shopping bag I hadn't noticed she was carrying and took out an old, worn packet of folded leather.

Sarah Byrne moved a step forward as Mary continued.

"I've been cleaning out my house and found this under the eaves in the attic, behind an old trunk next to the outside wall." She handed me the leather. "I'd like to know what it is. How old it is. And if it's worth saving."

I shook my head. "I don't know anything about old leather." I turned the piece over. Stains from traces of melted wax showed it had once been sealed against the elements. Or for privacy. "Did you open it?"

"I did. But almost all of the wax was already gone. I wasn't the first person to look inside." Mary's wide eyes were very blue, and very serious. "I hope I didn't do anything wrong."

"I already told you. That house is yours. You had a right to open anything in it." Rob shook his head impatiently and turned to us. "Mary's been sorting through a lot of old stuff. Mr. Fitch at the realtors' said her parents' house has to be cleaned out before we can sell it. We want to do that in September, when she's eighteen and has the deed." He glanced over at Mary. "Sorting everything is taking longer than we planned. Mary gets attached to things just because they belonged to her family."

Mary's cheeks flushed.

"No need to be embarrassed," I assured her. "This house has been in my family since the early nineteenth century. I feel the same way about a lot of things in it. Is your house old, too?" Haven Harbor was full of eighteenth- and nineteenth-century homes.

Without thinking, I touched the small gold angel I wore on a chain around my neck. Mama had given it to me "to keep you safe" on the day of my first Communion.

It wasn't valuable to anyone but me. But I still wore it often, for luck. And memories. Tonight I'd worn it so, in some way, Mama could see me hosting a dinner in our home. Could see I'd grown up.

If Mary was selling her house, her parents must not be around. I wondered what had happened to them.

She nodded, smiling a bit. "Built in 1770. No one's ever sold it out of the family." She glanced at Rob. "Not until now."

"Selling it must have been a hard decision, then," I said.

Mary was silent.

Rob answered for her. "People pay good money for old weather worthy houses. We sell it, and we'll be able to buy a lobster boat and maybe one of those new modular homes. A sternman's earnings aren't enough to cover a boat and a house." Rob gestured at the leather case. "Open it. You'll see why we're here."

"Come with me," I said, including everyone in the hall. "The light is better in the dining room."

I shooed Juno off the table, where she'd been cleaning tiny pieces of salmon off our plates, and cleared a space on the tablecloth for the leather packet.

Sarah reached over to stroke it. "It's certainly old. I'd guess over a hundred years. I wonder how long it's been in your attic."

"Go ahead. Open it," said Rob, impatiently. "That old leather isn't important. We're here because of what's inside."

"You look, Sarah. You're the expert on old things." I turned to Mary and Rob. "Sarah's an antiques dealer. She has a shop down on Main Street."

Sarah carefully opened the leather. It was cracked along its fold lines. Inside was a creased piece of cloth and a piece of paper. The paper had been folded over, and was brittle and stained. Sarah opened it carefully. "I should have cotton gloves on," she said, almost to herself. "I shouldn't be handling paper this old."

"I already touched it," Mary admitted. "I didn't think it was important. It's just an old letter. I couldn't even read it. The letters are faded, and I think it's written in French."

Sarah nodded as she bent down to look at the paper, careful to only touch the edges. Corners of the page had already crumbled, and the paper, like the leather that had protected it, had split along the fold line. "I don't think this is modern French. But you're right. It's a letter, signed 'Maria' or 'Marie.'" She raised her head and looked at the others in the room. "Do any of you read French?"

With Maine's centuries-old ties to Quebec,

many old-time Mainers spoke and read French. But no one here did.

Sarah refolded the note carefully and then opened the piece of cloth. "Wow."

It was a square panel of elaborate embroidery on fine linen damask. A cross-shaped design in the center enclosed an oddly shaped bird worked in heavy silk threads in tent stitch. Embroidered flowers were in the corners outside the cross. The details were in split and stem stitches in once brightly colored silk threads or metallic gold or silver with a border of small pearls.

I'd never seen anything like it.

"So, what do you think?" said Rob. "Is it worth anything?"

Sarah moved back so we all could see. The panel was about sixteen inches on each side. The awkward looking dove or pigeon was outlined in black and then embroidered in shades of red, blue, and gray. Silver threads were woven into his wings, and a few pearls were on his head. "A Byrd of America" was stitched above him.

The embroidery might once have been studded with more pearls, but the silk attaching them to the fabric was broken in several places. A green and red vine framed the whole piece, surrounding the faded flowers in the corners.

Sarah bent down to examine it more closely. "This is the first time I've seen anything like this up close. But"—she glanced over at me—"Angie and I've been reading up on old needlepoint. I'm pretty sure I've seen pieces like this pictured in books. If it's not a reproduction, it could date back to Elizabethan times. Nothing like this was done in the states or in Australia. And that 'Byrd of America' label probably means it was copied from a natural history book. It wasn't a bird the needlepointer was familiar with."

Whenever she mentioned her home country, Sarah's accent increased. I tried to hide a smile.

"'A Bird came down the Walk— / He did not know I saw— / He bit an Angleworm in halves / And ate the fellow, raw,'" she quoted.

Sarah also had the habit of quoting Emily Dickinson in odd moments. The needlepointers were used to that, but I saw Mary and Rob exchange a puzzled glance.

No one explained.

"That bird's not one I've ever seen," said Dave. "And I'm pretty good at recognizing North American birds."

"So, if it's old, that means it's valuable, right?" said Rob.

"It could be," Sarah said slowly. "But we'd need to do a lot of research to find out for sure." She turned to Mary. "You said your house was built in 1770. Was your family here before that?"

Mary shrugged. "I don't know. We've been here a long time. The men in my family were sea captains." She hesitated. "I assumed we came from England. Or Scotland. A lot of the original families around here came from the British Isles. I never heard my folks say they were from anywhere else."

"Would anything in your house give us a clue? An old Bible with family records in it? Diaries? Ships' logs?" Ruth leaned forward to get a closer look at the embroidery. "Old documents might hide clues about where your family came from. And where they acquired this."

Mary looked embarrassed. "I've found a lot of old books and papers. One old leather hymnal was cool, but I didn't recognize any of the hymns. A few ships' logs might be mixed in with the rest of the papers. My father had a stack of old papers in his desk, and there's a trunk in the attic full of leather books and loose papers. A lot are old schoolbooks. I didn't look at them closely. The papers were hard to read; many had been nibbled by mice. I didn't think anyone would be interested in old ledgers and textbooks." She glanced at Rob. "I've been trying to find any china or furniture or scrimshaw or pictures in the house that might be worth selling. My mom once told me the captains brought gifts home for their wives after they'd sailed to Europe and the Caribbean and Asia." She shook her head. "Mom and Dad died about two years ago in a plane crash. I never thought to ask them any more about family history. I wish I had."

"I'm sorry about your parents," I put in. Maybe that was why Mary was going to sell her home. She was closing that part of her life and moving on.

I silently hoped she was making the right decision. Mama had died when I was ten, and I'd never had a father. But, thank goodness, I'd still had Gram. And now I had our house. It hadn't been important to me when I was eighteen. Now I understood it was part of me, of my heritage. A part of my past I wasn't ready to discard.

"Don't throw any of those old books and

papers away," Sarah cautioned. "They might be important to you or your children in the future. Or they might help identify things like this embroidery. If you don't want them, you could donate them to the Haven Harbor Historical Society for safekeeping."

Sarah nodded slowly and moved back a step. "I have so many chests and boxes and drawers and wardrobes to go through. I don't have time to go through every piece of paper."

"I told her we should get a Dumpster," Rob put in.

Sarah winced. "It sounds as though you've taken on a major job, Mary. If you'd like help sorting through everything, I'd be happy to volunteer."

Mary nodded. "I'd like that. I don't know what's valuable or what's important to keep. A lot of things are old." She wrinkled her nose. "Some smell old. But so far I haven't thrown anything away. I've been sorting through the stuff and putting it in cartons in the living room or barn. Like, cartons for glass and china, and cartons for linens. And a couple for the old books and papers. I guess I need to look at the papers more closely."

"A lot of old houses along the coast used to be full of souvenirs of places Maine ships sailed. My ancestors were captains, too," I added. I didn't mention that many descendants of earlier Mainers had sold those things or given them away. Maine was full of antiques dealers and auction houses that had benefited from families who'd discarded those "old things," valuable and not valuable, and replaced them with modern equivalents. Not to speak of the treasures that had been unknowingly tossed into Dumpsters.

"So you think the embroidery is old?" asked Mary, getting back to her reason for being in my dining room.

Sarah shook her head. "I'm not sure. But even if it's a reproduction, it's certainly not twentieth century."

"A reproduction of what?" I asked.

Sarah hesitated. "I've been reading about Mary, Queen of Scots. This needlepoint looks remarkably like the stitching she did while she was being held in England."

"A queen did it? Then it's worth a lot of money, right?" asked Rob, grinning and clapping Mary on the shoulder. "We were right to come here."

"I don't know if Queen Mary did it," Sarah cautioned. "Her only known works are in museums in Scotland and England. But it might be from that period. We'll have to look at both the letter and the embroidery very carefully. We'd also have to establish provenance."

A queen's embroidery? Very unlikely. Why had Sarah even mentioned that possibility? It was cruel to get Mary's hopes up.

"What's provenance?" asked Mary, moving slightly away from Rob and keeping her eyes focused on Sarah and the piece of needlepoint.

"Provenance is the tracing of the history of the antique. Proving who owned it, and when. In general, the more important the owners have been, the more important the piece is." Sarah looked down at the leather case and its contents.

"Age is easier to establish if we know who owned the antique in the past, and how it passed from one person to another. This letter might provide clues. Other papers in your house would help us. Most important, assuming the embroidery isn't American, we'll need to figure out how it ended up in a Maine home."

"How would we do that?" said Mary. "I don't know where it came from, or when. Or who put it in my attic."

"Angie and I could help you try to figure it out," said Sarah. "That's part of what we do at Mainely Needlepoint."

Sarah didn't volunteer that so far we'd only taken on a few jobs of that sort. Usually we created new custom needlepoint for high-end stores or decorators. We'd restored several pieces of vintage embroidery, and with the help of a lot of reference books, we'd helped a woman from Castine identify three samplers she'd bought at an auction. But those samplers had all been from nineteenth-century New England. I suspected identifying this embroidery would be a lot harder.

The history of needlepoint was complicated. I'd been studying books about nineteenth- and early twentieth-century needle crafts. I never thought we'd be asked about a piece of embroidery earlier than that. But Sarah, who was more fascinated with European history than I was, had been reading about earlier stitching. Thank goodness, I thought, as I listened to her talking to Mary.

We might be able to guess at an approximate

date for the embroidery. But could we go further and establish provenance? It seemed a long shot.

"If you'd like us to take this on as a project, we'd be happy to find out as much as we can about it," Sarah was continuing. "You'd have to trust us with the packet and its contents for a little while, while we do the research."

"And we can't promise we'll learn much," I added.

Mary looked reluctant. "I thought the stitching was pretty. Rob's mom was the one who said I should have it checked out. Then Ethan said you folks were experts on needlework. Will you need to keep it very long?"

"If it's valuable, how can we trust you to keep it safe?" Rob asked. "What would keep you from selling it and saying you'd lost it?"

Maybe, having a state trooper for a brother, Rob'd heard too much about crime scenes. Or he just wasn't very trusting. This needlework had been hidden in an attic for decades—maybe a couple of hundred years—and he was worried about Sarah and me losing it?

I swallowed my anger. He might not have meant to insult us. "If the embroidery and the case and letter were in a safe, would you feel more comfortable?"

"I guess so," said Mary hesitantly.

"I'll write up a note saying you've entrusted us with the embroidery. We'll all sign as witnesses. Then tomorrow morning I'll take the embroidery to my grandmother's lawyer, Lenore

Pendleton." I looked from Mary to Rob and back. "Do either of you know her?"

"Her office is here in Haven Harbor, right?" Rob asked hesitantly.

"Right across from my house, on Pleasant Street," volunteered Dave.

"I know her," Mary said, to my surprise. "She's my lawyer, too. She helped me after my parents died. Helped fix it so I could live with my friend Cos's family after my parents died and not have to go into foster care."

Rob looked aggravated. Maybe he'd thought he knew everything about his fiancée.

"I'm glad, Mary," I said. "I'll ask her to hold the packet and the embroidery and letter until we know for sure what they are."

Mary nodded. "I hope you can find out who it belonged to. It's fun to imagine a woman sewing that hundreds of years ago. And it would be awesome if a queen made it!"

"Yes," I agreed. "It would be. But we don't know that. Don't even tell anyone that's a possibility until we figure it all out. We wouldn't want to get people all excited and then find out we were wrong."

"We'll do our best," said Sarah, touching Mary's arm. "And we'll do it as quickly as we can."

"And if it's worth a lot of money, then you could help us to sell it," said Rob.

"No," said Mary, softly but firmly. "That embroidery must have been important to someone in my family, for it to have been hidden so long. We'll see what Angie and Sarah find out about it. But it should stay in my family."

Chapter 3

Up to the time of the War of the Roses English Embroidery was justly famous, but it then languished, and when the taste for it revived it was never again executed with the same amount of gorgeous simplicity, the patterns becoming too overloaded with ornament for true taste.

—Sophia Frances Anne Caulfeild and
  Blanche C. Saward, *The Dictionary of Needlework: An Encyclopedia of Artistic, Plain and Fancy Needlework,*
  London, 1882

I wrote a simple statement describing the letter and embroidery and packet, stating it belonged to Mary Clough, who'd asked Mainely Needlepoint to identify its age and origin. Mary and I signed and dated one copy for each of us, and then Rob, Dave, Sarah, and Ruth signed as witnesses.

If the needlepoint did turn out to be valuable, I didn't want anyone questioning who owned it, or what our responsibility for it was. I wasn't worried about Mary. But Rob hadn't hidden that he was more interested in money than in provenance or family history.

By the time Rob and Mary left we didn't have time to eat dessert before the fireworks started at nine. While Dave and I quickly piled the dirty dishes in the kitchen sink, Sarah and Ruth examined the embroidery again.

"It does look Elizabethan," I heard Ruth say. "But I'm no expert. I didn't want to say anything when those young folks were here. They were excited enough with your mentioning Mary Stuart."

Sarah nodded. "You're right. I should have held my tongue. But the primitive bird would definitely fit the Elizabethan period. And two of the flowers are a primitive thistle and a rose."

Dave went in and peered over their shoulders. "Symbols of England and Scotland? That should help in identifying the work."

"Unless the person who did the embroidering just liked those flowers. We don't know anything yet," I put in. "But it would be exciting if it were four or five hundred years old."

"Exciting, for sure," agreed Sarah.

"But unlikely," added Ruth. "Not many pieces of fabric or embroidery would be in as good condition if they were Elizabethan."

"Even if they were in a sealed packet?" I asked.

"A packet sealed once," agreed Dave. "When it was intact the wax would have protected it, kept the air and dampness out. But the seal had been broken. Who knows? It could have been broken two hundred years ago."

"Or ten years ago," I said.

Ruth turned her walker toward the front door. "Well, it's a mystery to me. And fascinating. But nothing we're going to solve tonight. Angie, your dinner was wonderful, but I'm feeling my age. Would you feel insulted if I asked to take a piece of your pie home with me? I'd hate to miss a piece of strawberry-rhubarb. The arthritis in my hands keeps me from doing much baking these days, but I do love desserts. I can sit upstairs and see the overhead fireworks from my bedroom window while I'm indulging."

"I'll drive you home," said Dave. "But only if Angie'll give me a piece of pie, too."

"I'll fix you each a piece to go," I promised, opening the pantry door to find heavy paper plates. "I can't eat a whole pie. How about you, Sarah?"

"I'd still like to see the fireworks," said Sarah. "And then come back here later for pie?"

"Good. Because I'd like to go down to the waterfront. I haven't seen Haven Harbor fireworks since I was in high school."

I cut generous slices of pie and wrapped them for Dave and Ruth.

"I'll walk out with you and carry the pie to your car," suggested Sarah.

Dave nodded agreement as he helped Ruth slowly start for the front door.

"I'll put the embroidery away while you're doing that," I agreed.

"Thank you again for the supper. It was delicious. I haven't had a traditional New England Fourth supper in years," Ruth said as she and Dave left.

I watched as he helped her and her walker get down the three steps from my porch to the walk. Then I went to get the embroidery.

It was beautifully crafted, although the outline of the bird used as a pattern was still visible and some silver threads were broken. Could it be as old as Ruth and Sarah wondered?

I tucked the packet and letter with the embroidery into one of the bureau drawers in Gram's front hall. The drawer next to the one where I'd hidden my gun.

No one would break into the house on the Fourth of July and steal a piece of embroidery.

Many Haven Harbor residents left their doors unlocked during winter months. Most families had known their neighbors for years. Burglaries were rare. But this time of year the town was filled with tourists. Doors were locked more often, just in case. The majority of people from away were good folks, and their credit cards were critical to Haven Harbor's economy. But "better safe than sorry," as Gram would say.

And I'd promised to keep the packet and its contents safe.

"Ready to head down to the waterfront?" I grabbed my sweater from a chair in the living room and pulled it on. Maine days were beginning to warm up. This evening the temperature would probably be in the fifties, with chilly sea breezes.

Sarah nodded, and we started down the hill toward the harbor.

Most Haven Harbor stores, including Sarah's, were on Main Street. A few were on Wharf Street, the parallel street that ran along the working waterfront. Light was fading. Stores normally were closed by this time of night. But not on the Fourth of July.

The fireworks display was a time to attract tourists (and local folks) to restaurants and gift shops. Tonight almost every store was open, from the hardware store to the patisserie to the bookstore. A table outside one of the gift shops was piled with "Haven Harbor, Maine" sweat-shirts, hoping people from away would realize being comfortable on a July evening in Maine would require more warmth than their shorts and T-shirts supplied. One enterprising young man had set up a stand on the way down to the town pier to sell mosquito repellant.

Not a bad idea. I remembered fighting off swarms of mosquitoes while watching fireworks years ago. Tonight, though, the stiff sea breeze should keep biting creatures away.

On how many Fourth of Julys had I walked the distance from our house to the waterfront to see the fireworks? Some years, when she hadn't been waitressing, Mama and I had gone to-gether. After she'd disappeared I'd been with

Gram, or with one or another of my friends. The last few years I'd been here I'd been working at the lobsterman's co-op on the pier, steaming lobsters for summer folks and glancing up at the fireworks over my head.

On days like this one, memories of growing up in Haven Harbor haunted me. Other days, the memories were good ones. Good and bad times were all mixed up in my head.

I glanced into the Harbor Haunts Café as Sarah and I passed. "Want to stop for a drink after the fireworks?" I suggested.

"And miss your strawberry-rhubarb pie?" asked Sarah.

"I can bring you a piece tomorrow morning," I assured her. "I have to take the needlepoint to Lenore Pendleton's office anyway."

"Pie for breakfast sounds good," she agreed. "One of my favorite Maine customs. Sure, we could stop at Harbor Haunts on our way back. But it'll probably be crowded. And we each already had several glasses of wine with dinner."

Several glasses of wine? I hadn't noticed.

Crowds already filled the streets that connected Main Street to Wharf Street, and then to the piers. "Let's go to the beach. We should have a good view from there," I suggested, raising my voice so Sarah could hear me as we wove in and out of vacationing and local families, young couples blissfully unaware of blocking the sidewalks, and older couples letting the world pass by.

Sarah nodded and we turned right, toward

Pocket Cove Beach, the small rocky beach between the piers on the waterfront and the lighthouse. Mama had always taken me there to see the fireworks.

We weren't the only ones heading in that direction.

When I was little the annual display was set off from one of the Three Sisters, the small uninhabited islands that sheltered Haven Harbor from the sea. One year someone—certainly not the harbormaster—decided they should be launched from a barge in the harbor itself. The coast guard hadn't been thrilled with that idea. Nor were the people who'd hoped to have a good view of the display from their boats and, instead, were showered by falling embers.

In those days fireworks were only set off by professionals. Now anyone could buy fireworks. I suspected the Haven Harbor Hospital was prepared for burned fingers tonight. I hoped nothing worse would happen.

But I wasn't worried enough to miss the show.

"I wish Patrick were here," Sarah said a bit wistfully as we squeezed our way through the throng to find a good viewing spot near the far end of the beach. Families had been there for hours, staking their claims with blankets and beach chairs and coolers of food and beer or soda. We found a small space on the rocks to sit near the western end of the beach, where it curved toward the lighthouse.

"How's he doing?" I asked. Patrick and his

mother, actress Skye West, had bought an old Victorian house in Haven Harbor last month and were restoring it. Unfortunately, Patrick had been burned in a fire that destroyed the carriage house he'd hoped to make his artist's studio. "Wasn't he planning to come back to Maine for physical therapy?"

"That's still the plan," agreed Sarah.

She'd been attracted to Patrick since the day they'd met. I'd been interested, too. How could a woman not be? He seemed like the whole package: good looking, kind, and even had money. But Sarah had spoken first, and he seemed to have made his choice. I was in touch with his mother, since she'd asked us to reproduce several needlepoint pillows of local birds. Dave had taken on that project. He'd already finished the puffin and was working on the laughing gull. I hadn't heard directly from Patrick since his accident.

"Mass General wants him to stay in the burn unit a little longer. He needs more skin grafts."

I shuddered. "I hope he'll be able to come back soon." And that he'd still be able to paint, I added to myself. Patrick's hands and arms had been badly burned.

"He seems to think so," said Sarah. "His mom had hoped to be here this week, to check on the construction at their house, but her agent insisted she meet him in California. She had a meeting about her movie that starts filming in the fall."

Clearly Sarah was keeping in touch with both Patrick and his mother.

"Oh, and he said to wish you a happy Fourth. I told him I'd be having dinner and seeing the fireworks with you."

So he hadn't totally forgotten me.

The sun was setting. Purple and orange streaks filled the sky, and were reflected in the harbor.

"'And still within a summer's night / A something so transporting bright / I clap my hands to see,'" Sarah quoted as we watched the sun go down. The fireworks tonight had competition from the brilliant sunset.

The tide was low, but brisk breezes blew incoming waves farther up the beach than usual. Excited voices calling back and forth to friends and family covered the sounds of the water and wind.

I remembered standing in this spot, holding Mama's hand. I'd loved the colors of the fireworks, but hated their loud noise. One year she'd brought my winter earmuffs with us on the Fourth, hoping they'd muffle the sound. They hadn't. People near us had pointed and laughed. I've never seen a pair of earmuffs without remembering that Fourth of July.

The first flares to go up were blood red. My mind went to other places, other times. The next flare was white, sending ghostlike tentacles across the sky. If I hadn't been with Sarah I'd have turned and headed for home. I'd felt relaxed and happy today. I hadn't thought about the past. I didn't want to remember. But Sarah was smiling and clapping with the crowd.

The third flare was an exploding blue chrysanthemum that turned the dark night sky a color I'd only seen in postcards of Caribbean waters. North Atlantic waters were deep blue gray or even black, on stormy days.

Sarah nudged me. "Aren't they wonderful?"

I nodded. "Wonderful." I didn't tell her the images they'd brought to my mind. Images I hoped would soon fade, as quickly and as completely as the fireworks themselves. Mama'd been gone since I'd been ten. I needed to forget the empty days without her; remember the earmuffs and the warmth of her hand tightly holding mine.

My life was going on.

The crowd around us was "oohing" as the fireworks increased in size and complexity and number. Finally the last display filled the sky with colors, drowning out the cheers of the spectators and pushing my thoughts back into the past. We stood there until the last pinpricks of color mixed with the stars.

"Time for that drink?" Sarah asked.

We turned and followed the crowd toward the center of town.

"Definitely," I agreed. I could use a strong one. Why were good memories sometimes harder to deal with than bad ones?

"Let's get together tomorrow to talk about Mary Clough's embroidery," Sarah added, as the crowd swept us back up the hill, like a school of fishes pulled in by the tide. "When you bring me that piece of strawberry-rhubarb pie you promised."

The Harbor Haunts Café was open year round, and in winter months was a comfortable place to meet friends, get warm, and sip a hot toddy. On this Fourth of July night it was crowded with people I didn't know commenting on the fireworks and the weather (only a visitor from away would say the weather was chilly on the Fourth) and asking for brands the bartender didn't stock. A few small tables were outside, for the overflow crowd, but most people were packed in by the bar.

"Beer?" Sarah called. She'd managed to maneuver herself closer to the bar than I had.

"Fine," I called back. Beer was my usual. I wasn't picky about the brand.

"Two Shipyards," I heard her order. "Summer Ale." I moved next to the wall, where there was a little more space. Or, I'd thought there was space. My arm bumped Nicole Thibodeau, one of the co-owners of our local patisserie. "So sorry," I said, seeing her white wine dripping down the front of her sweatshirt. "This place is incredibly crowded."

"No problem," she answered, wiping her chest with a napkin. "I was only going to have a few more sips before I headed for home anyway. If I'm lucky, all these people will crave croissants in the morning. This is our first big week of the season."

"Where's Henri?" I asked, looking around for her husband.

"Not here," she said wryly. "So I'll be up way

before dawn tomorrow. Poor Henri's mother has Alzheimer's, and on top of that, two days ago she had a stroke. He went to see her. He's talking to the doctors; seeing if she'll be well enough to go back to assisted living."

"I'm sorry," I said, waving at Sarah, who was trying to make her way through the crowd to me carrying our two beers. "Does his mother live far from here?"

"Quebec," Nicole answered. "A five-hour drive. Too far to visit on a daily basis, or even weekly, especially in the tourist season. We haven't seen her often since we opened the patisserie here four years ago. The store is demanding. Now Henri's saying we should move her here, to be close to us. But medical costs in the US are so much greater than in Canada."

I nodded. "That makes it difficult for all of you. Tell Henri I'll be thinking of him."

Nicole nodded. "*Merci.* I'm worried about her, of course. She's almost ninety. But I'm hoping Henri can come back and start baking again in a day or two. Fourth of July week means nothing in Quebec. Here, it's crazy time."

I reached for the cold bottle Sarah held out and took a deep swig.

"Hi, Nicole," said Sarah. "Was Angie telling you about our little challenge?"

"*Non*; I've been telling her of mine," said Nicole. "What challenge?"

"We've been asked to identify a piece of embroidery. It's old, and may be valuable." Sarah leaned over toward Nicole and lowered her voice. "It looks Elizabethan to me."

"*Vraiment?*" said Nicole. "That's fantastic."

"A note written in French was with it. We don't know for sure the note is connected to the embroidery, but we need to have it translated," Sarah explained, her voice rising a little as the noise of the crowd increased. "Do you think you could take a look at it for us? Translate it, if you could? If the note's as old as the embroidery might be, it wouldn't be in contemporary French."

"*Mais oui,*" Nicole answered immediately. "Such a thing could be very valuable. I would be delighted to help. But are you in a dreadful hurry? Because Henri is out of town, and I shouldn't even be here now. I should be back at the patisserie."

"When Henri's back, then," I agreed. "And thank you. I'm going to ask Lenore Pendleton to hold the note and the embroidery for us, so nothing happens to them. Before I take the note to her I'll make a copy for you."

"Bring it down to the patisserie when you get a chance," said Nicole, reaching around Sarah to add her empty glass to a tray near the door. "Henri should be home in two or three days. At least I hope so!"

"Our best wishes to his mother," I added, as Nicole nodded and headed for the door.

"Henri's not here?" asked Sarah.

"His mother had a stroke. He's with her in Quebec. Nicole was a little panicked about the crowds she'll need to bake for this week. I'm glad you thought to ask her about that note. I'd already forgotten about it."

"I was just reminded," said Sarah, trying to stay steady on her feet in the crowd.

"Look who's over at the bar."

I craned my head to see, but Sarah was taller than me. "Who? Liam Neeson?"

"You wish! No—Rob Trask. He's with Ob Winslow's son, Josh, and Arvin Fraser."

"Is Mary with them?"

"No. But Jude Curran, that new hairdresser at Maine Waves, is. And a pretty young woman with long dark hair and tight jeans who looks Indian. Or Pakistani."

"Not that you noticed."

Sarah grinned. "Actually, I noticed because I heard one of the guys say 'needlepoint.' Of course, he could have been discussing his latest sewing project."

"Likely. Didn't we tell Rob not to talk about it?"

"We did. But that was a couple of hours ago."

I shook my head. "Nothing we can do about it now. Rob said he was a sternman. He may work for Arvin. This place is too crowded," I added as a tall man maneuvered his way between us. "There's no room even to stand."

I drained my beer, and Sarah nodded and put her half-empty bottle on the tray. "Let's get home."

I left her at the door to her store and apartment with a promise to see her in the morning, bearing strawberry-rhubarb pie, and headed back up the hill alone.

The night was black, the town lit only by the full moon and the stars. Haven Harbor had installed a dozen streetlamps down on Main

Street, but as soon as I'd left the commercial area I could have used a flashlight. I usually carried one in my pocket or bag, but tonight I'd only planned to be out for half an hour or so. I'd stuck my keys and a few dollars in my pocket and left everything else at home.

My porch light was welcoming. So was Juno, who rubbed herself on my legs as soon as I got inside.

I'd never had a pet. But since Gram's wedding I'd understood why she'd adopted one. Having a cat meant you didn't come home to an empty house, even if you lived alone.

Juno would be moving to the rectory with Gram. Maybe I should think about getting a cat or dog of my own.

In the meantime, Juno reminded me of my responsibilities. She led me to the kitchen and let me know she could use fresh water and a few treats. I obliged. Gram was going to have to put her on a diet when she got home, but I couldn't resist Juno's purrs.

The dishes piled in the sink could wait until morning. I decided I could use a drink and a treat, too. I got a beer from the refrigerator, cut a piece of the strawberry-rhubarb pie, and sat down at the kitchen table.

Juno jumped onto my lap and checked out what I was eating. I scratched behind her ears and then put her down. "Juno, it's just you and me again. But this is my dinner, not yours. Happy Fourth of July."

She purred in acknowledgment.

Despite the mixed memories, it had been a

good evening. The food and company had been fine, and the fireworks dramatic. And now Mainely Needlepoint had a new job. I'd have to start working on that in the morning.

Why hadn't Rob Trask been with Mary tonight? If he'd been my fiancé I don't think I would have been pleased at his leaving me on July Fourth to go drinking with his buddies.

But who was I to judge? I didn't have anyone to snuggle with tonight except Juno.

Chapter 4

Old Mother Twitchett had but one eye,
And a long tail which she let fly
And every time she went through a gap
A bit of her tail she left in a trap.

—Traditional English riddle/nursery rhyme

My telephone woke me the next morning. "Gram?"

"Tom and I were thinking of you last night. How'd your dinner party go?"

I sat up in bed. "Really well. Your advice on baking the salmon was perfect. How's the honeymoon going?"

"We've been sightseeing, mostly. Been to a couple of wonderful museums. Now we're checking antiques shops for Ouija boards Tom can add to his collection and local galleries and craft stores to find a perfect souvenir to bring home. Not that we'll need anything to remember this trip! And we're overindulging in French food. I may come home ten pounds heavier. I could become addicted to drinking a bowl of hot chocolate for breakfast, even in July."

"Yum. Sounds great!"

"We'll be home in a couple of days. Tom has to preach next Sunday."

"Don't cut your trip short. Enjoy yourselves."

"Don't worry. We are. Anything else new?"

"One thing. We have another piece of needlepoint to identify."

"Yes?"

"Two young people stopped in last night. Rob Trask, Ethan's younger brother, and his fiancée."

"Mary Clough?"

"You know her?" Silly question. Gram knew everyone in town.

"I've known the Cloughs all my life. They're one of the original Haven Harbor families. Mary's the only one left in town now. Her parents died a couple of years ago and she moved in with the Currans to finish high school. You've met Jude, their oldest daughter."

Jude Curran. She was the girl Sarah had seen at the Harbor Haunts with Rob and Josh and Arvin.

"She's one of the hairdressers at Maine Waves," Gram continued. "She's a couple of years older than Mary. Cos Curran is closer to Mary's age. They've been best friends since they walked to elementary school together."

Now I was sure. Jude was the twentyish hairdresser with the curly red hair who always wore an orange coverall at the salon.

"Mary must be seventeen or eighteen by now, though," Gram continued. "Near old enough to take ownership of the house she inherited."

"Eighteen in September," I said. "And planning to sell it."

"Sell! Out of the family? That's a big decision to make at eighteen. I'd heard she and Rob were engaged. She's young, but maybe she's looking for a new family. Someone to take care of her. The Trasks are good people. I hope she's made the right choice. I don't know why she and Rob wouldn't live there, in her house. Rob still lives with his parents."

"They want to sell her house so Rob can buy a lobster boat. They're planning to get a smaller place to live in."

The silence on the other end of the line told me of Gram's disapproval. "I hope she knows what she's doing. With the history that house has . . ."

"What about the history?" I asked. "Of the house, or the family? Knowing the history might help us identify the needlepoint Mary's found."

"She hasn't told you?" Gram said. "I know young folks aren't as interested in their heritage as they might be. But that family has a fascinating history, if my memory serves. You pay attention to anything she's found in that house." She paused. "My husband is telling me to get off the phone now. He's actually found a list of galleries we haven't visited yet, and he's anxious to get started. I'll fill you in on the Cloughs when I get home if you haven't heard it all by then. Love you!"

The history of the Clough house? If Mary wasn't sure about it, who would be? I'd worry about that later. First I needed to get myself up and out of bed. Dirty dishes were waiting for me in the kitchen.

As was my second piece of pie, along with two cups of coffee. Juno padded back and forth, following me from the dining room to the kitchen as I put everything from the party away except for the piece of pie I'd promised Sarah.

Then I carefully photographed the leather packet, the letter, and the needlework itself, with close-ups, printed them out, and made copies. The first set of copies I added to the "Mary Clough" file I'd started with the contract/receipt we'd all signed last night. Thank goodness for the convenience and speed of computers and digital cameras.

I could have photographed the items last night and returned them to Mary, but Sarah or I might need to examine them more closely once we were close to figuring out what they were. Plus, I'd had a hunch Rob might have tried to sell the needlepoint even before we'd figured out its story. He'd been a bit too interested in its value, not its history.

Mary herself might decide to sell it. But she should be the one to make that decision.

Not that it was any of my business.

When I'd been her age, ten years ago, I was sure whatever I was feeling would never change. That if I didn't make a decision immediately, I'd never have another chance.

I'd taken every dime I had and left Haven Harbor behind. I wasn't heading toward a specific place or person. All I knew was I wanted to get out of town, get out of a place where everyone knew me and my mother, and judged us both. I wanted a fresh start.

If I'd owned this house, or the things in it, then, would I have sold them? I might have, I admitted to myself. But I'd been lucky. I'd had Gram. I hadn't appreciated her then. I hadn't realized Gram was looking out for the future me.

Now I didn't care what my house or its contents were worth to the world. I valued this place, and all it contained, for who'd lived here, and for the memories it held, good and bad.

I hoped Mary wouldn't be pushed into making a decision she'd regret. Holding the needlepoint for a few days, or even weeks, might help her think through what she wanted to do with it.

Of course, she was in love, and especially at seventeen, love was more important than anything else. Especially to a girl who didn't have a family.

I slipped the leather packet and its contents into a padded envelope, cut a generous slice of pie for Sarah, and headed down to Main Street.

Chapter 5

A cool-looking summer bedroom-set consists of bureau-scarf, pincushion cover, bedspread and bolster-cover of unbleached muslin with patches of pink morning-glories, green leaves, and stems, and bands of pink, all of light-weight sateen.

—*The Modern Priscilla*, May 1918.
  The Modern Priscilla was a monthly
  magazine for women published
  between 1887 and 1930.
  Its editorial focus was on needlework
  and everyday housekeeping.

Summer had arrived in Haven Harbor. Gulls soared above the boats and buildings, screeching messages to each other. Tourists, easily identifiable by their shorts, souvenir T-shirts, and cameras, filled the sidewalks, looking in shop windows and, even at nine-thirty in the morning, standing in line to buy saltwater taffy or locally made ice cream.

Most of the shops, including From Here and There, Sarah's business, were already open. This was the high season. The time of year when people in Haven Harbor made (or didn't make) the money that would keep them going through the winter. The more hours your business was open, the more possibilities for sales.

Her shop's nineteenth-century brass doorbell rang as I pushed the door open. A man wearing jeans and a Disney World shirt was looking through a shelf of salts.

The world of antiques was new to me. Maine had always been full of antiques shops and auction houses, but they hadn't been part of my life when I was growing up.

Now Sarah was a friend, and I was trying to learn a little about her business. I'd never heard of salts or saltcellars until Sarah'd shown them to me. Now I knew they were little bowls that elegant families from Roman times to the early twentieth century put at each guest's place to hold individual portions of salt (with tiny spoons to match the place setting). The "master salt" was a larger bowl of salt for the table, or for refilling the individual salts. She'd assured me people collected them, especially the Victorian crystal patterned salts. I couldn't see the attraction. But I was learning there was a collector for everything.

Her potential customer didn't even look up when I opened the door.

I waved at Sarah and headed toward her

counter. "As you ordered," I said, handing her the slice of strawberry-rhubarb pie. Sarah grinned and tucked it under the counter.

"I've been waiting for my breakfast," she said, keeping her voice low. "I'll eat it as soon as I can." She glanced at her potential customer meaningfully.

Customers came before breakfast. No argument about that.

I held up the envelope I was carrying. "I'll stop at the patisserie and leave Nicole a copy of the note that was with the needlepoint. She's probably too busy to look at it this morning, but maybe she'll have time later. Then I'm heading to Lenore Pendleton's office."

"Good plan," Sarah agreed. "Last night I pulled out several books on Elizabethan needlepoint, but I haven't had a chance to look at them yet." She gestured at a stack of books on the other side of the counter.

"Do you really think it's that old? That's the fifteen hundreds, right?"

She nodded. "I was excited about that possibility last night, but I'm feeling more realistic this morning. Did you bring me a photo of the needlework?"

"Thanks for reminding me." I opened the envelope and pulled out the copies I'd made for Sarah. "When I get home I'll check my books on old needlepoint, too. And Gram called this morning. After I told her about Mary she said the Clough family and their house have a long history. She didn't have time to say more."

"I was surprised Mary didn't know more about her family," Sarah said. "Family history fascinates me. I'd love to know more about where I came from."

Sarah'd never said much about her background. I'd wondered what brought a woman in her early thirties all the way from Australia to Maine. All she'd ever said was she'd come to New England because of her love for Emily Dickinson's poetry, and found Haven Harbor.

Dickinson had lived in Amherst, Massachusetts . . . not exactly next door to Haven Harbor. I suspected there was more to Sarah's story. I hoped someday she'd tell me more.

"I guess Mary didn't care about things that happened a hundred years ago. Or before her parents died she wasn't old enough to think about anything but being a teenager. Now there's no one to ask."

"Maybe," said Sarah. She kept glancing at her potential customer. "I should ask him if he has any questions about the salts," she whispered. "Call me when you have a translation of that note."

Chapter 6

My next stop was the patisserie. I'd decided to treat myself to an éclair for dessert tonight. I was hoping Nicole would also have a couple of baguettes left. Gram had given me one of the two panini presses she'd gotten as wedding gifts. I was looking forward to making a classic ham and cheese sandwich to test my new toy.

The store smelled sinfully of fresh bread and frostings and fruit fillings.

A dangerous place for anyone worried about

sugar and carbs. But I refused to worry. Life (and that included food and drink) should be enjoyed.

I wasn't the only one who thought so. I could see why Nicole had been concerned about Henri's absence. Half a dozen people were either waiting in line or checking the pastry case before making their decisions. I didn't know the young woman behind the counter; she must have been a summer hire. I gave her credit. She looked frazzled but kept smiling.

Two éclairs were in the case. Clearly they were both meant for me.

I got in line behind a woman holding a drooling baby wearing a pink onesie printed with "Daddy Loves Me."

A shirt I never could have worn. I hoped that little girl knew how lucky she was.

When I got to the front of the line I placed my order and asked, "Is Nicole here?"

"She's in the kitchen. Busy," said the young woman, putting my choices in a box and a bag.

"Would you give her this, when she has a few minutes?" I scribbled a reminder to Nicole and my telephone number on a copy of the French note. "Last night she said she'd try to translate this for me."

The girl nodded. "I don't know when she'll have time to look at it."

"That's okay. Just make sure she gets it."

"I will," she said, handing me my change. "Have a good day."

I planned to. Right after I delivered the embroidery to Lenore Pendleton's office.

Like the Mainely Needlepoint office, which was in our living room, Lenore Pendleton's law office was on the first floor of her home, a classic white colonial. Mainers called them "four on fours," because they were square, and originally had four rooms on each floor. Over the years many had been modified by the addition of conveniences like closets and bathrooms, but the basic structure of most of the houses, and their outside appearance, hadn't changed.

Dave Percy's little yellow house was catty-corner across the street. I'd forgotten that.

I hoped Lenore wouldn't mind my volunteering her safe. In the two months I'd been back in Haven Harbor I'd met her a couple of times. First, to ensure that everything connected with Mama's death had been done properly, and then, recently, Gram and I'd consulted her about how to transfer what I still thought of as Gram's house to me.

As I turned up Lenore's brick walk a heavyset man in a badly fitted suit stormed out her door, slammed it behind him, and stomped past me. He got into a beige sedan and gunned it.

Someone was having a bad day.

I opened the door to the front hall and walked into the reception area. Lenore's secretary, Glenda Pierce, wasn't there, so I obeyed the "ring bell to let me know you're here" instruction on the desk, and rang her small enameled brass bell.

Within a few minutes Lenore appeared in the doorway between her office and the reception area. Her brown hair streaked with gray was clipped up, but a few strands had escaped and were curling down her neck. She reached up to secure them as she walked. "Angie! I didn't expect you this morning. Your appointment isn't until next week."

"I took a chance your office would be open." I liked Lenore Pendleton. She was friendly but professional. The last time I'd seen her she'd suggested I make out a will. I'd thought it was only something you'd do if you were a lot older than twenty-seven, or if you had children. She'd convinced me otherwise. I had an appointment with her next week.

"From nine to five, almost every day," she said, giving up on her hair. "I played hooky yesterday because of the holiday, and told Glenda she could take the week with her family. But there's always paperwork to catch up with. You know what it's like to have your business in your home."

"You never leave your office," I agreed.

"But there are real advantages when the weather turns horrible. Come on in," she said, gesturing to the private office in back of her reception area. "Your grandmother's wedding was lovely, by the way. She and Rev. Tom looked so happy. Are they still on their honeymoon?"

I nodded. "They're in Quebec, eating so much they'll be wanting to hibernate when they get back, according to Gram."

"Sounds like Charlotte," said Mrs. Pendleton. "I hope she and Tom are happy together."

"So far, so good," I agreed. "Marriage seems to be right for them."

"Perhaps so," she said. "But the tough part of marriage comes after the honeymoon."

I didn't know what to say. "I've never been married."

She saw me glancing at her left hand. "I'm separated. Filed for divorce eighteen months ago. My advice about marriage is simple: don't rush into it. In my profession I see a lot of couples who marry too soon. Or who think getting married will solve all their problems."

"I think Gram and Tom are old enough to know what they're doing." Gram was sixty-five; Tom, fifty-two. They'd each been married before. Gram'd been widowed years ago, before I was born, and Tom about ten years ago. I hoped they'd have many years together.

Mrs. Pendleton brushed her hair up again. "Of course they are. I shouldn't have said anything. It's just that marriage and divorce have been on my mind recently. What's brought you here this morning?" She straightened the line of books on her desk, pushing the marble bookends that held them more toward the center. They'd been dangerously close to falling off the edge.

"You know Mary Clough, right?" I asked.

"I helped her with legal issues after her parents died. She's a sweet girl. Horrible tragedy, to be left alone so young."

"Last night she came to my home with her fiancé . . ."

"Her fiancé?" Mrs. Pendleton looked shocked. "Mary's engaged?"

"To Rob Trask," I said.

Lenore shook her head. "She's so young. I hadn't heard. Sorry to interrupt."

"That's okay," I said. "She does seem young to be engaged. But in any case, she brought a piece of needlepoint for me to identify. It may be several hundred years old."

"Interesting," said Lenore, leaning forward.

"Mary wanted to know more about the needlepoint, and how much it might be worth." I hesitated. "Rob seemed most interested in its value."

"It might be worth a lot?"

I shook my head. "I don't know. I've never seen a piece like it. We'll have to do research. But it's possible."

"What brings you here?"

"In case it *is* valuable, I want to keep it out of harm's way. Secure." I didn't add "and away from Rob." "Mary agreed that, if you wouldn't mind, we'd leave it with you. You know both of us. And you could put it in your safe." I held up the envelope. "It wouldn't take up much room, and I hope you wouldn't have to keep it more than a few weeks. It could only be days."

She nodded. "Most people would use a safe deposit box. But I could do that for you. I assume you don't want the responsibility of having it in your home."

"Exactly. And I don't have a safe deposit box."

"May I see this embroidery?"

"Of course." I opened the envelope and took out the leather packet and then the letter and the stitching. "The needlepoint and this note were inside the leather."

Mrs. Pendleton didn't touch any of the pieces I spread out on her desk. She just looked at them. "You're right to keep them safe. That needlepoint is exquisite."

"No matter how much we find out it's worth, it's definitely special," I agreed.

"You said Mary knows her needlepoint will be with me?"

"Yes."

She leaned back. "Put everything back in the envelope, then. I'll put it in my safe, I promise. And I won't release it to anyone but you or Mary. No matter who asks."

Chapter 7

Mutual happiness our mutual object. May the cares that bind the covetous never disturb our peace. May we yield therefore one to another and be equally yoked in the command of God.

—Stitched marriage certificate between
Reuben Dade, age twenty-two, and
Lucinda Brooks, age sixteen, 1821,
Gloucester, Massachusetts

My new panini press worked beautifully. I carried my sandwich and a glass of lemonade out to our porch to eat. Sunny July days shouldn't be wasted.

After I finished I tossed the crumbs from my sandwich to the sparrows holding their daily meeting at our front yard bird feeder.

I'd been so busy preparing for Gram's wedding, and then for my dinner party, that I'd gotten behind in paperwork for the business. I turned on my computer and starting sorting through invoices.

The afternoon went quickly. Office work wasn't my favorite kind, but my in-box was finally empty and I had a stack of envelopes ready to mail.

I was about to have an end-of-day beer when Ruth called.

"Angie, I wanted to thank you again for the lovely dinner you prepared last night. I so enjoyed getting out a bit and seeing everyone."

I made a mental note to keep more closely in touch with Ruth. She was the oldest of the needlepointers, and her arthritis kept her from doing much stitching. At her request, I hadn't given her any jobs recently. But there must have been days when she felt isolated in her home. Spending time online wasn't the same as being with other people.

"I've been thinking about that needlepoint Mary Clough showed us last night. You and Sarah are the experts on old needlepoint." I rolled my eyes. I wished I were an expert. But Ruth was still talking. "But I know a little bit about it, too, and I've always loved English history. When Sarah said last night she thought the stitching might be Elizabethan, it got me to thinking. So I spent time online this afternoon."

"Yes?" I said.

"I may not be right. In fact, I keep thinking I couldn't be right. But what Sarah said was true. That embroidery square looks very like other work by Mary, Queen of Scots."

"Do you think so?" I blurted. "I meant, it's old

stitching. But . . . royal?" I'd convinced myself
that, at best, the needlework was a copy.

"Maybe not, maybe so. But check it out. That
stitching and the work Mary Stuart did have a lot
in common. She was famous for her needlepoint, you know."

So I was learning. Yesterday I didn't know
that. In fact, I still wasn't sure who she was.

"You said queen of Scots. So she was Scottish?"

"Oh, my dear, yes. She became queen of Scotland when she was six days old. When she was
five years old she was promised to Francis, the
Dauphin of France, and sent to France to learn
French and the customs of their court. She and
Francis married when she was sixteen. A year
later his father, the king, died. Francis became
king of France, and Mary, his queen. But a year
after that, Francis died of an ear infection. Isn't
it awful what people died of years ago? So Mary
went back to Scotland with two titles—queen
of Scots and dowager queen of France. She had
a claim to the English throne, too, as a descen-
dant of Henry VII's sister. That's why her
cousin, Elizabeth—Queen Elizabeth the First,
of course—kept her under lock and key for so
many years."

No, I didn't know all that. And I got a little
lost trying to follow Ruth's story. My semester on
world history at Haven Harbor High hadn't
covered much. And, to be honest, I hadn't paid
much attention. But I did get Ruth's basic
message: this Queen Mary had been pretty
important in Elizabethan times.

"She was in prison?"

"Not a dungeon, of course. After all, she was a queen. But Elizabeth was afraid Mary's supporters would try to put her on the English throne. She'd already been thrown out of Scotland because she'd made poor decisions choosing her two husbands after Francis—she wasn't good at relationships, I always thought—and she was Catholic. Scotland was Protestant then. So Mary asked her cousin Elizabeth for asylum. Elizabeth offered her a place to live at the home of the Earl of Shrewsbury, one of the lords who supported Elizabeth. But when Mary got there she found there was a catch. She couldn't leave. And she could have very few visitors."

"So she was all alone there?"

"Oh, she was allowed to bring a few members of her staff with her, including her ladies-in-waiting and her chef. And the earl's wife, Bess of Hardwick, became a friend of sorts, as well as a jailer."

"How long was she held there?"

"Eighteen years. And then she was put on trial for treason, found guilty, and beheaded."

"Whoa. Not a pretty ending."

"No. But what's important to us is that Mary'd learned needlepoint when she was a child in France. Like other women of her station, she had professional needlepointers working for her, designing and stitching tapestries and bed hangings and elegant clothing. But she and her ladies also did needlepoint themselves. It helped fill those long years of exile from Scotland and imprisonment in England."

Locked up eighteen years, without even a television set or a newspaper. Needlework might seem pretty important if it was all you could do. "But even if the needlepoint Mary Clough showed us is Elizabethan, how would we know who stitched it?"

"Noble ladies like Queen Mary stitched their own emblems, or symbols, or even their initials, into their work. The books you and Sarah have about Elizabethan needlepoint should picture those."

"I'll let Sarah know," I assured Ruth. "She's doing most of that research. I still think it's a long shot. How would a queen's embroidery end up in a Maine attic?"

"Let me know what you discover," said Ruth. "I love mysteries."

Could Ruth be right? If a queen's embroidery had ended up in Maine, it would probably be worth a lot. But, how could we find out? I was pretty sure stitching by Mary, Queen of Scots, didn't go on the market often.

Ruth didn't get excited about very much. But she'd sounded convinced.

What if I'd held a piece of needlepoint stitched by a queen?

I shivered. I felt as though a ghost from the past had reached out and touched me.

Chapter 8

In the end is my beginning. (En ma fin est mon commencement.)

—Motto of Mary, Queen of Scots (1542–1587), referring to the phoenix, the emblem of her mother, Mary of Guise

I kept thinking about Mary, Queen of Scots. She'd been sent out of Scotland when she was five to grow up in another country, speaking another language. Living at the French court must have been as good as life got in those days. But being there hadn't been her choice. And then she'd been married when she was sixteen and widowed at seventeen.

Most childhoods (then and now) were pretty simple compared to hers. Mary Clough might be a little young to be engaged. But at least she'd chosen her future husband.

When I was about five I'd been obsessed with princesses. Clearly I'd had the Disney versions in mind.

Interesting though Ruth's story had been, I couldn't believe a queen's embroidery had ended up under the eaves of a Maine attic. It didn't make sense. But the possibility was fun to think about.

I started going through Gram's books on needlepoint. I needed to find out more about the Elizabethans.

Turned out Gram had a lot of books on the stitchery of that period. She even had a book on Mary Stuart's needlepoint. I put that book on top of the pile, but didn't open it.

It had been a long day. I was heading for the kitchen to get a beer and forage for something to eat other than the last piece of strawberry-rhubarb pie when Sarah called.

"Have you eaten yet?" she asked.

"I was just thinking about that," I answered.

"Me, too. Plus, I wanted to get caught up. Did Lenore Pendleton agree to hold Mary's embroidery for us?"

"She did. And I dropped a copy of the note in French at the patisserie for Nicole to translate. I haven't heard back from her yet, but she was busy today. Did that man this morning buy any of your salts?"

"He was intrigued, but not enough to pull out his credit card. Today was a museum day. Lots of lookers, lots of questions, not many sales. I did sell a framed map of the district of Maine from 1816, though. That was a good sale."

"I'm glad."

"Since you haven't eaten either, I wondered if you'd like to splurge and meet me down at the co-op for lobster."

I hesitated. But not for long. When I'd been in high school I'd spent all my summer days at that lobsterman's co-op, steaming lobsters and clams and mussels and corn for anyone who wanted to sit outside on the wharf, look at the harbor, and celebrate a classic Maine day. The job hadn't exactly been a glamorous one.

I was beginning to appreciate Maine seafood from the other side of the steamer.

"Sure. I could do that. Meet you down there in about twenty minutes? That'll also give me a chance to tell you about a call I got from Ruth."

I pulled on a light jacket and headed down to Wharf Street. The evening was still warm, although afternoon breezes had cooled the air. Barn swallows swooped low, finding insects for their chicks. In the distance a laughing gull cried, and several crows called to each other. A murder of crows, I thought to myself as I took a deep breath of salt air.

I'd been back in Haven Harbor two months now. On days like this it was hard to believe I'd endured the burning summer heat of Mesa, Arizona, for ten years. The flat desert and adobe walled yards and pink and aqua accents seemed like a movie I'd once seen. Another world.

Sarah got to the co-op first. She'd already bought each of us a beer and was saving one of the picnic tables on the wharf. "You've done the hard part," I said, looking around. Finding a picnic table at the co-op during the first week in July was like finding a pearl in your oyster. "I'll order our food. What do you want?"

"The special—pound and a half soft-shell lobster, steamed clams, and corn."

"Got it." That wasn't hard to remember. It was the most popular order at the co-op. I'd have the same. I stood in line at my old steamer to place our order. The line was longer than I'd hoped. By the time I got back to our table Sarah'd almost finished her beer. I'd catch up with her quickly. "I'll get us two more," I volunteered. "Our dinners won't be ready for at least fifteen minutes."

I headed for the small co-op bar, where the selection was beer, inexpensive white wine, or sodas.

Sarah had finished her first beer by the time I got back to our table with her second.

She leaned forward across the table. "Look in back of me. Over by the railing. That's Rob Trask, with Josh Winslow and Arvin Fraser, right? The three guys who were at the Harbor Haunts bar last night. Jude Curran and that other girl from last night are with them, too."

The co-op and Harbor Haunts were the only restaurants (except for the yacht club's dining room) in downtown Haven Harbor. I wasn't surprised to see the same people two days in a row. "They're looking down at the float. Probably complaining about today's boat price and congratulating Arvin for being a co-op member. And, you're right. That other girl's a stunner."

"Boat price?" Sarah looked puzzled.

"The price lobstermen get for their catch when they deliver it to a wholesaler. It changes every day, and lobstermen always complain about it. But, of course, co-op members don't use a wholesaler. They bring their catch here, to be sold at the restaurant or, uncooked, sold by the pound on the other side of the wharf. By running their own operation they make more profit." Facts of lobstering I'd grown up knowing.

"They've been standing there for the past ten minutes," Sarah said softly, glancing at the five near the water.

"Arvin has a lobster boat. Probably Rob is his sternman," I pointed out. "Josh works for anyone who needs an extra hand when he isn't helping out with Ob's fishing charter. Most likely they're talking lobsters."

"With a girl from away?" Sarah looked askance. "If neither of us recognizes her, then she isn't from Haven Harbor."

"Maybe she's with Josh," I said. "Since Arvin's married and Rob's engaged."

Jude was there, too. I wasn't sure I wanted to know the intricacies of all their relationships. Besides, they could all just be friends.

I felt a little protective of Josh. His dad, Captain Ob Winslow, was one of the Mainely Needlepointers. I knew Ob and Josh hadn't seen eye-to-eye during the past couple of years, after Josh dropped out of college and was fired from a series of jobs. But this summer Josh was back home. Ob had confided proudly that the boy—he was in his early twenties—was finally settling down. The *Anna Mae*, Ob's fishing charter, only

went out when it was booked, though, so
sometimes Josh had time on his hands. This
wasn't the first time I'd seen him hanging
around the docks with the guys he'd grown up
with, many of whom now made their living from
the sea.

A sternman made twenty percent of the pro-
ceeds from the day's catch. Not a dependable
income, but on a good day it would buy a lot
of beer.

As I watched, the group left the railing and
headed for the bar. A few minutes later they
sat down at the table in back of Sarah with a tray
of beers and a pile of French fries.

When I'd worked here the lobstermen had an
unwritten rule that they wouldn't sit in the
restaurant area, especially at this time of day.
They were taking seats that might have been
used by customers. Besides, lobstering was smelly
work. Sitting next to a Maine lobsterman might
be a little too much reality for the noses of out-
of-staters.

It didn't seem to bother the young women
with those three guys tonight.

And maybe the rules had changed. Maybe
now lobstermen didn't drink their beer or eat
their hamburgers (few ate lobsters—that was
business) in the office of the pound. Those five
didn't seem to mind letting several groups wait
for a table.

"When we were on the telephone you said
Ruth called," prompted Sarah.

"Thanks for reminding me. She spent the afternoon on the Internet," I said. "She sounded

pretty convinced that you were right: the embroidery Mary brought us last night might have been done by Mary Stuart. Mary, Queen of Scots, she was called."

"Good to hear she didn't think I was crazy," said Sarah. "I didn't have as much time as I'd hoped today—all those customers who wanted to talk, but not buy, took up a lot of time. But I did confirm that in Elizabethan England and France, and probably other European countries as well, women copied the wood engravings in books on the natural history of Europe and the Americas. The book illustrator drew a bird or animal based only on a written description; he'd never seen the actual subject of his drawing. Today it's hard to tell what species he was trying to illustrate."

"And women used the drawings as patterns for needlepoint?" I asked.

"They did," Sarah confirmed. "And although illustrated natural history books were rare and expensive, certainly Mary, Queen of Scots, would have had access to them."

I had to lean in a bit to hear Sarah. The men in back of her were talking louder and gesturing more dramatically. I suspected they'd been drinking before they'd sat down, and the plastic glasses of beer on their table were beginning to disappear into the wooden trash barrels at the end of their table.

Rob's voice rose above the rest. "Stick with me, Josh. In a few months I'll have my own boat and traps. I have my eye on a thirty-five footer down in Boothbay. It's a beauty. Only a couple of years old. The guy who owns it is leaving the business. When I'm set up, you can be my stern-man."

"You planning on winning the lottery?" Josh answered. "One of them boats costs a pile. Couple of hundred thousand dollars, counting the engines and all the gear."

"I've already practically won the lottery," said Rob. "I've got it all figured out. Mary's going to sell that old house of hers, and all the stuff in it. Some of the junk she's found may be worth a lot." His voice lowered only slightly as he added, "I told you last night. She has a piece of cloth with stitching on it that might be four hundred years old. Maybe five hundred. Hell, I don't know. That little cloth might be worth a major down payment on a lobster boat." Rob raised his beer glass to everyone at this table.

Arvin Fraser shook his head. "Don't count your bugs until you have the traps, Rob. Houses can take years to sell. Besides, all that stuff belongs to Mary. She might not be thrilled to put all her money into a boat. Women can be funny that way. I can tell you, being married doesn't mean doing what you want to do. Not even before your wife up and gets pregnant on you."

Sarah raised her eyebrows. We both kept listening. It wasn't hard—the guys' voices kept getting louder.

"Mary'll do what I tell her to. Don't worry about that," Rob said confidently.

Arvin's voice was louder still. "Josh, if I were you I wouldn't quit working for my dad. Rob's dreaming."

"You wait and see," said Rob. "I know what I'm doing. Maybe the house will take a while to sell. Who wants an old house anyway? But that embroidery thing—that could sell fast, and for big bucks." He turned to the young dark-haired woman, whose voice was so soft I couldn't hear her. "Right?"

"Who'd be interested in buying an old piece of cloth?" said Arvin.

"Probably an auctioneer would take it. They know stuff about antiques," said Rob. "Or someone who works for a museum." He raised his glass toward the young woman again. Her back was to me, so I couldn't hear what she was saying, if she was saying anything at all.

"Auctioneers and museum folks. You know a lot of those," Josh taunted. "Don't worry, Arvin. I'm not quitting my gig with you. I'll sign on with Rob when I see his boat."

"You think you're smart," said Rob. "But I already know a museum in Boston that's interested. And they haven't even seen it yet."

Sarah and I looked at each other. "He's talking about Mary's embroidery," she said quietly.

I nodded. "He must be. But . . ."

"Number forty-seven" boomed the loudspeaker that announced dinners were ready.

"That's us," I said, getting up. "You keep

listening." I pulled out my wallet and headed for the pickup window to get our tray of food.

A museum interested in the needlepoint? He must be bluffing. We didn't even know how old that embroidery was. Or who'd done it. Or how it had gotten into Mary's attic.

Rob was already planning how he'd spend the money they'd get for it.

He'd better have an alternate plan for financing that boat.

Chapter 9

*Medieval embroidery is another popular fancy.
It is done in crewells, or fine Berlin wool . . .
the designs are, as the name infers, from old
tapestries. They are traced on linen by means
of transfer paper, and then a line is worked
round the margin in black chain stitch, and each
petal or portion of design is filled up with chain
stitch in one shade. The stalks are made by using
double crewel and bringing the needle out between the two threads. The work is very durable,
and is handsome and easily done.*

—S. Annie Frost, *The Ladies' Guide to
Needle Work, Embroidery, Etc.*, 1877

By the time I got back to Sarah with our dinners
Arvin and one of the girls had left. Rob, Josh,
and Jude were talking to an older couple sitting
at another table. They were too far away for us to
overhear their conversation.

"What was that all about?" I asked Sarah. "Did you hear Rob?"

"He was talking through his hat. I can't believe he'd think the embroidery would be worth as much as a lobster boat and gear." Sarah shook her head. "And talking as though the money was almost his! Even *if* the embroidery is worth something and *if* Mary wanted to sell it and *if* she could find a buyer . . . it would be her money. Not Rob's."

"You heard him."

Sarah shrugged. "That's beer talking."

I looked around her. "He and Josh and Jude are still talking to that other couple. I don't know them." Not that it was any of my business. But I was curious.

Sarah intentionally dropped one of her napkins and glanced over her shoulder. "I know them. They're antiques dealers from Canada, Victor and Oriel Nolin. They were in my shop this afternoon looking for nineteenth-century paintings and prints."

"Do you carry those?" I asked, thinking of Sarah's shop. She'd hung a few old prints and paintings on the walls, but I hadn't paid much attention to them.

"I had a half dozen Bartlett steel engravings of Quebec and Montreal. They were pleased. Said Bartletts of Canadian places sell well for them."

"Good sale, then," I said.

"When they were paying, Mrs. Nolin saw my stack of embroidery books in back of the counter. She asked if I had any old needlework to sell, or knew anyone who did. She has a customer interested in samplers and old needlework."

"Why come all the way to the states to buy?"

"The exchange rate is on their side now. And the Nolins said they stay in Haven Harbor when they come to Maine for an auction or to check shops. They're friends of Henri and Nicole Thibodeau."

"Did you sell them any samplers?"

"I only had one. Mrs. Nolin wasn't interested because it was dated 1924. Her customer wants older pieces."

"Too bad."

Sarah shrugged. "It happens. At least they bought the Bartlett engravings. Visitors to Maine aren't interested in pictures of Montreal or Quebec. The Nolins left me their card in case I found anything Canadian. Their gallery is in the old part of Quebec City. I'll file their names." She turned and looked at the couple again. "I wonder how Rob knows them."

"Maybe they took one of his dad's fishing charters. Better he talk to them than be bragging to his friends." I started cracking my lobster's claws.

For the next few minutes we focused on our food.

"How's your lobster?" Sarah asked. "Mine's the best I've had this season." She dipped a piece of claw into her melted butter.

I finished sucking the sweet meat out of one of the legs. "Delicious. Can you believe this is the first steamed lobster I've had since I've been home? Not the first lobster, of course. Skye West kept us well supplied with lobster rolls when we were working at her house last month."

"When we've been here before you've always ordered fried clams."

"I do love clams fried well," I admitted. "Chewy, not crispy. Not greasy. And in light batter."

"I always figured Mainers said they didn't like lobster to show their innate superiority to those of us from away." Sarah grinned and started in on her claws.

"Possibly," I agreed, as we settled in to serious, messy eating. "But I do like lobster. Especially soft shells, or new shells, as people call them now, even if the hard shells have more meat in them. But it's not the only seafood I like."

"Soft shells are easier to eat than hard shells," Sarah agreed, slipping her lobster's tail out of its shell.

I sipped my beer and then swooshed a steamed clam in my broth. "You're probably right about Rob's trying to look like a big man in front of his friends. But it burns me that he's not only positive Mary will fund his lobster boat, he's even telling other people about it."

"Mary has to learn to stand up for herself. She chose him. She must know what he's like. It's nothing to do with us."

"I hope she's not just marrying him because it's a familiar direction for her life to take. That she thinks he'll take care of her."

"That may be," Sarah agreed. "She's young and alone. And Rob's not a bad-looking guy and comes from a decent family. All that's good.

You can't expect her to wait until she's as old as your grandmother to get married!"

I laughed and tossed a piece of shell in her direction. "You're right about that. But here . . . I'm twenty-seven, and you're what . . . thirty-two?"

"Thirty-three, actually. But don't share it with everyone here," Sarah answered complacently. "And, I know. Neither of us are married. Or even engaged."

"Still looking," I said with a straight face.

"Haven't found the right guy," she countered.

"Need my space."

"Don't want to give up my dreams for someone else's."

We both laughed. "That last one may not be Mary's situation. She may not have any dreams beyond being married."

"Sad. I hope that's not why she chose Rob."

I smiled at Sarah. We were both joking about marriage. Sarah'd fallen hard for Patrick West last month. And me? I'd fallen for lots of guys. More guys than anyone knew. But I'd never fallen all the way.

A couple of those guys might even have been the right ones. I hadn't let them be.

The temperature was dropping; I was glad I'd put on a light jacket. Sarah was digging the last little pieces of meat out of her lobster's body.

"Did you have lobsters in Australia?"

"Not like these."

"You've certainly learned how to eat them."

She grinned. "When in Maine . . ."

"Speak the language and eat the food."

We wiped our hands with the packets of wet wipes the co-op had put on our tray, and dumped the empty clam and lobster shells in one of the trash barrels. Overhead a squabble of gulls screeched and dove toward us, hoping for a feast. We closed the top of the barrel before they reached us.

Maine days are long in early July. But they're already losing sunlight a minute or two each afternoon, on their way to the darkness of December and January.

Now the sun was setting, sending streaks of orange and pink and purple over the Haven Harbor lighthouse as we trudged back up the hill to our homes, full of beer and seafood.

"It will be hard to know exactly how old that embroidery is, won't it?" I asked.

"Beyond the point of knowing it isn't new, it would involve chemical analysis of the threads and dyes," agreed Sarah.

I nodded. "Things we're not equipped to do."

"The Museum of Fine Arts in Boston might be able to do the tests. Or the Museum of Textiles in Lowell, Massachusetts. I can't see us attempting them. We don't want to injure the work."

"So the best way to get an idea of how old it is would be to establish—what is that word again?"

"Provenance. The history of an item—who owned it through the years. By establishing provenance, we'd also get closer to the age of the embroidery," Sarah agreed.

"Before I start doing a lot of research on Mary's family, I'd like to talk with her again. Without Rob. See what she wants us to do."

"Sounds like a good idea," said Sarah, turning in at her store. "I'll keep reading up on old embroidery. Let me know if you find out anything helpful, though."

"Of course." I said good-bye and headed up the last two blocks to my home.

It had been a busy day. I didn't plan to make it a late night. I'd call Mary tomorrow.

Chapter 10

Nuns' work: Crochet, Knitting, Netting, Cut Work, Drawn Work, Pillow and Handmade Laces, Satin Embroidery and Church Embroidery were at one time all known by this name. From the eleventh to the fifteenth century the best needle-work of every kind was produced by the Nuns, who imparted their knowledge to the high born ladies who were educated in their convents, and from this circumstance each variety, besides being distinguished by a particular name, was classed under the general one of Nuns' Work.

—Sophia Frances Anne Caulfeild and
   Blanche C. Saward, *The Dictionary of
   Needlework: An Encyclopedia of Artistic,
   Plain and Fancy Needlework*, 1882

The next morning I spent a little quality time with Juno, who was missing Gram and wondering why I wasn't giving her twenty-four/seven attention.

Her immediate wants were satisfied by a round of "find the catnip mouse" and part of a can of sardines. She promised not to tell Gram about the sardines.

I called Mary and left a message. Could we get together to talk about her family history? Anything she knew or even vaguely remembered might help. I was especially interested in the people who'd lived in her house, but if she knew anything about connections to Scotland or England (I also threw in France, because the note was in French), that might help.

If the embroidery had gotten to French Canada it could have gotten to Maine. The "Canada Road" along the Kennebec River to Quebec had been well traveled since the American Revolution, when Benedict Arnold had (incorrectly) assumed it would be an easy path to attacking the British in Quebec City.

I might not know a lot about British history, but Haven Harbor schools had made sure I knew Maine history. Prints of Benedict Arnold and his weary men, many of them ill with smallpox, trying to make it through heavy December snows to Quebec, had hung in several of the classrooms I'd been imprisoned in during my school days.

Nicole hadn't gotten back to me about the translation of the note. I wouldn't bother her about it until Henri was back home. She'd said it might be a couple of days.

I spent an hour calling the gift shops Mainely

Needlepoint worked with to see if they needed
to reorder any more balsam pillows or wall hangings. A couple did, so I called Dave Percy and Ob
Winslow to ask them to stitch up more of our
best sellers. Dave was just about finished with the
pillow covers for Skye West and said he'd start on
the small pillows next. Ob's wife, Anna, said he
couldn't take on any assignments now; he was
out fishing on the *Anna Mae* almost every day.
Sarah was researching the antique needlepoint,
so Katie Titicomb was next on my list. She was in
Blue Hill visiting her grandchildren, but said
she'd be able to do a few pillows. Pillows didn't
bring in as much money as our custom work, but
they got our name into the hands of people who
might call us later.

I was taking a coffee break on the porch when
two police cars headed down to the harbor. A
shoplifter? Then the Haven Harbor ambulance
followed them. Neither the police cars nor ambulance had their sirens blaring.

I wondered what was wrong. I wasn't worried.
No sirens meant no emergency. Maybe someone
had slipped on one of the wet docks. Or had
chest pains. I hoped no one'd drowned. In a
harbor town that happened once in a while, especially when kids, or people ignoring the
dangers of rock climbing, slipped on the rocks
near the lighthouse and fell into the powerful
surf. Being thrown against jagged rocks made
swimming difficult, if not impossible. Every few

years someone died there. Usually someone from away.

I went back inside and returned to my phone calls. Whatever the problem was, it had nothing to do with me.

Or so I thought.

Chapter 11

While idle drones supinely dream of fame
The industrious actually get the same.

—Verse stitched on sampler by Sally Alger
 at Miss Polly Balch's School in
 Providence, Rhode Island, 1782

The next time I saw a police car it was parked in front of my house.

Sergeant Pete Lambert from the Haven Harbor Police Department was standing on my porch. With him was Ethan Trask, a detective with the Maine State Troopers Homicide Unit. Rob Trask's big brother. The one who'd suggested Rob and Mary bring her needlepoint to me. The one guy in town I wished wasn't married.

"What happened? Is it Gram?" Those two wouldn't be paying me a visit unless the circumstances were dire. Had Gram or Tom had an accident? Was she ill? Before either of the men could open their mouths I'd imagined ten or twelve horrible scenarios.

"Your grandmother's fine, Angie," said Pete. "But we have a situation we're hoping you can help us with."

A situation? When Ethan Trask was involved a "situation" usually included a body.

"May we come in?" Ethan asked. Ethan's smiles could make me blush, even if he were commenting on the weather. No danger of that now. This morning he wasn't smiling.

I opened the screen door and pointed toward the living room. Then I remembered my manners. "Iced tea or lemonade?" Gram would have been proud of me.

Then I realized who it must be. If Gram was fine . . . "Is Tom all right?"

"Sit down, Angie," said Ethan. "We don't need any drinks. And relax. This time your family is fine."

This time. Two months ago Ethan had been the one to tell me the details about Mama's death.

I nodded. "So. What happened?"

"You know Lenore Pendleton, the lawyer," said Pete. "You're one of her clients, right?"

"She helped with Mama's estate. I have an appointment with her next week to draw up a will."

Pete and Ethan looked at each other.

Ethan spoke next. "Afraid you're going to have to find another lawyer, Angie. Lenore Pendleton is dead."

"Dead!" I was waiting to hear bad news. It

never occurred to me it would be about Lenore. "I saw her . . . yesterday."

"That's what we're here to talk to you about," said Pete. "We found a note on her desk with your name on it."

"What did it say?"

"Nothing. Just 'Angela Curtis,'" said Ethan. "Almost a doodle. The kind of note you write to yourself to help you jog your memory. We're here to find out when you last saw her, or talked with her, and why."

"She didn't die of natural causes, did she?" I said, looking from one of the men to the other. Neither of them said anything. "Ethan, I'm not stupid. The State of Maine doesn't send a homicide detective to investigate a natural death."

He hesitated, clearly debating what to tell me.

"No, we don't think she died of natural causes. But it won't be official until after the medical examiner's report. Now, when did you see her last?"

"Yesterday morning, at her office. I got there a little after ten o'clock."

"Was she alone?"

"A man was leaving as I went in," I remembered. "Her secretary, Glenda, wasn't there. Lenore said she was on vacation. So, yes. She was alone."

"Who was the man who left?"

"I didn't know him. He was middle aged, graying, with a bit of a potbelly. Wearing a cheap suit. What I remember most was that he didn't look happy. He slammed the door as he left, and then stomped down the stairs and the walk."

I tried to remember. "He drove off in a beige car. Fast." I mentally thanked the years I'd spent doing surveillance in Arizona.

Pete and Ethan exchanged looks.

"Do you remember what make the car was? Or its license plate number?" Pete asked.

I shook my head. Unless I was on a "follow and photo" assignment I didn't write down every license plate number I saw.

"How long did you stay at Mrs. Pendleton's office?"

Today Ethan's eyes were even bluer than usual, reflecting his blue shirt. "Fifteen, twenty minutes. Not long."

"Lawyer-client relations are private. But would you mind telling us why you were there?"

"It wasn't private or personal. I'd been given a piece of antique needlepoint by a client. You know about that, Ethan; you were the one who referred Rob and Mary to me."

"Mary Clough's needlepoint?"

Pete looked up from his note taking.

"Yes. I thought the stitching might be valuable. I asked Lenore to keep it in her safe while I was investigating it."

"Did she agree to do that?"

"Yes. She agreed to put it in her safe."

"Did she know it belonged to Mary Clough?"

"I told her it was Mary's. Lenore promised she wouldn't let anyone have it except Mary or me."

"So if anyone else came to her office and asked her for it, she wouldn't have given it to them. She wouldn't have opened her safe."

"No. She wouldn't have." I looked from one to the other. "What happened to Lenore? What has this to do with Mary's needlepoint?"

"How many people knew you were taking the needlepoint to Lenore's office?"

I tried to be patient. "Mary Clough, and your brother, Rob. Sarah Byrne. Ruth Hopkins and Dave Percy. Oh, and I told Gram when I talked with her on the phone yesterday morning." I hesitated. "Of course, any of those people could have told someone else." Like Rob had told his buddies. But Rob was Ethan's brother. No reason to call attention to him.

"No one else?"

"Who else would care?" I said. "Now, would you tell me what happened?"

"We don't know exactly," said Pete. "This morning Rob went to Lenore Pendleton's office with a friend, intending to show his friend the needlepoint. They found the door to Lenore's house unlocked and Lenore lying on the floor of her office. Dead."

Chapter 12

Behold the Savior at thy door
He gently knocks, has knocked before
Has waited long, is waiting still
You treat no other friend so ill
Admit him or the hour's at hand
When at his door denied you'll stand.

—Hymn 326 from *John Dobell's Collection.*
Stitched on sampler by eight-year-old
Martha Baldwin in 1820,
Newark, New Jersey

"How was she killed?" I had to ask.

"We won't know officially until the medical examiner tells us. But, unofficially, she'd been hit on the head," Ethan said. "Multiple times."

"Hard," seconded Pete. "Probably with a marble

bookend. It had blood on it, so it's going to the lab."

I cringed a little. How could anyone do that? Or, more correctly, *why* would anyone do that? "When did it happen?"

"The medical examiner will have to make that call. For now we're guessing early this morning," said Pete.

"Or very late last night," Ethan added.

"How was she dressed?" I asked.

Pete and Ethan exchanged glances.

"She was wearing a nightgown and robe. An open box of pastries was in her kitchen. We're thinking she might have been having a late snack when she had an unexpected guest. It may have been a robbery gone bad," said Ethan. "Her safe was open, and empty."

"Empty? Everything was gone?" I repeated.

"Not everything. Files were scattered on the floor," explained Pete.

"Was a padded envelope among the files? Sarah's embroidery was in a padded envelope."

Ethan shook his head. "Nothing like that. No padded envelopes. No needlepoint. Glenda Pierce, Lenore Pendleton's secretary, has agreed to go through the remaining files to see if any are missing. But the needlepoint was gone, and so was jewelry Glenda said Lenore kept in the safe. Most of the jewelry was Lenore's; a few pieces belonged to one of her clients. Glenda's putting together a list of the jewelry that was there."

Glenda wasn't having a relaxing vacation week after all.

I tried to focus on Lenore's death, but all I could think of was that the needlepoint I'd promised to keep safe had disappeared. It was my fault. I should have kept it in my own house.

"Was the lock on the door broken? Or the window?"

"No," said Pete, although Ethan looked at him sharply.

I'd been able to help the police before, so Pete sometimes told me details civilians shouldn't know. Ethan didn't approve.

"So she knew whoever killed her. No woman would have opened the door wearing her night-clothes if she hadn't known the person outside."

"Angie, we're not asking for your advice on this case. We wanted to clarify your connection to Lenore," said Ethan. "So, you didn't see her or talk to her after you left her office at about ten-thirty yesterday morning?"

I shook my head. "No. Did Lenore handle criminal cases?"

Pete was more flexible about answering. But he wasn't in charge. He was with the Haven Harbor Police. He might help out in a murder investigation, but Ethan, with the state police, was the boss on homicide investigations. "None I know of. Her specialty was family law—wills, divorces, settling estates, adoptions. She'd been in town for . . . how many years do you think, Ethan?"

"She was here when I was in high school. I re-

member going to her office to have her husband
notarize a document for me. Charlie ran her
office in those days." Ethan paused, figuring. "So
she's been here close to twenty years. She must
have opened her office right after she passed the
bar." Ethan had grown up in Haven Harbor.
That's why murders in town were assigned to him.

"Her husband used to be her secretary?" I
asked.

"You could put it that way," Ethan agreed.

"Lenore told me she was separated. That
she'd filed for divorce," I said.

"Yeah. She kicked Charlie out two or three
years ago." Pete looked over at Ethan as if for
confirmation. "Story I heard was he'd lost a lot
of her money when the stock market went down
a while back. Started drinking about then, too.
We picked him up a few times for a D and D."

"Drunk and disorderly," Ethan added.

I nodded. I knew what a D and D was.

"Charlie's a nasty drunk." Pete shook his
head. "He's spent a couple of nights with us."

"Where's he now?" I asked. I didn't know the
man, but he sounded like a logical suspect.

"We'll be checking on that. Last I heard he'd
rented a place out of town and was looking for
work."

A woman I'd known and respected had been
killed in her own office. If Lenore's killer hadn't
taken any files, he or she must have been looking for the jewelry in her safe. The padded envelope might have looked as though it contained

more jewelry. Someone looking to fence jewelry wouldn't know about needlepoint—or care about it. They might toss it in a Dumpster once they saw it.

"I have photos of Mary's needlepoint," I said, getting up and opening my file on Mary Clough. "If the jewelry was valuable enough to be kept in a safe, I assume you'll be looking for it. I hope you find the needlework, too. I can't imagine an average thief thinking embroidery was valuable."

"Beats me why they took it," Pete agreed, taking the pictures of the needlepoint and the packet and letter. "But thanks for this. We'll add it to the list of missing jewelry Glenda's working on and send the descriptions to the usual pawnshops and jewelers. Who knows? Maybe we'll get lucky."

"You don't sound optimistic," I pointed out.

"The guy who did this may not have planned to kill anyone. But he did, and that's where the focus of our investigation will be—on finding whoever killed Lenore Pendleton. Finding the missing jewelry is important mainly because it might lead us to the guy who did this," explained Ethan.

I wasn't surprised. He was a homicide detective.

"It didn't look like a professional job. And Lenore was hit by something in her office—she wasn't shot or knifed. So it was a crime of opportunity. The crime scene folks are down at her office now, checking for DNA and fingerprints.

And the ME's report will help. At this point, we're just establishing a timeline." Ethan got up. "Thanks for the pictures of the needlepoint, and for telling us about the man you saw leaving Lenore's office. Whoever he was, if he was that upset, he might have returned later."

Pete turned as the two men headed for the door. "If you think of anything else that might help us, you know where we are."

I nodded. I did. In the two months I'd been home I'd been all too closely in touch with both of them.

They were almost to their car when I did think of something else. I ran down the slate walkway to the street. "Pete?"

He turned toward me. "Yes?"

"Are you going to tell Mary Clough about this?"

She'd be upset. And I'd rather be the one to tell her than have her hear through the grapevine, or from Rob. Law enforcement people weren't supposed to talk about cases, but word gets around fast in small towns. Probably half the people in Haven Harbor had already heard about Lenore's murder. And, after all, Rob was Ethan's little brother.

"She's not on the top of our list. We don't expect she'd break into Lenore Pendleton's office and kill her to get her own property back," said Pete with a small smile.

"Then it's okay if I tell her? I feel responsible for her losing her needlepoint."

He shrugged. "Up to you. But it was just

sewing. I'm more worried about the reactions of whoever's jewelry was stolen."

Just sewing. But what if it were sewing worth a small fortune? Or the down payment on a lobster boat?

I had to tell Mary what had happened.

Chapter 13

And thou shalt make an hanging for the door of the tent, of blue, and purple, and scarlet, and fine twined linen, wrought with needlework.

—Exodus 26: 36

Mary hadn't returned my call from yesterday, but this time she answered right away. She was at the Currans' house, where she'd been living since her parents died. She sounded surprised that I wanted to see her now, but she explained where the house was and agreed I could stop in.

I didn't mention what had happened to the needlepoint. I wanted to tell her that in person.

She wasn't going to be happy.

The Currans' house was smaller and more contemporary than most in Haven Harbor. I couldn't date it—I know more about target shooting than architecture—but I'd guess early twentieth century.

Sarah answered the door.

Gram would have said the living room was "decorated in cozy." Flowered slipcovers on the chairs and couch, Hummel figures in a glass cabinet, a large braided rug on the floor, and afghans thrown over the couch. The furniture faced a flat screen TV.

Mary was wearing black yoga pants and a loose T-shirt from the botanical garden in Boothbay. Her shirt, and one of her cheeks, were smudged with dust.

"Come in." She opened the door wider. "I was working at my house this morning, but I usually come home to have lunch with Cos. And Jude, if she's not working. We just finished. You've met Jude?"

I nodded. "At Maine Waves. Hi, Jude."

"How's Charlotte?" she asked.

"Gram and Tom are still on their honeymoon. They'll be back tomorrow or the next day."

"Tell her, if she needs her hair done, to call ahead. We're a little shorthanded with summer people here. And we're short one hairdresser."

"I'll tell her when she gets home," I assured Jude.

"And this is Cos," Mary said, pulling her friend forward. "She's been my best friend forever."

BFF. People really said that? Cos was a younger and shyer version of Jude, with hair still its natural brown. She smiled at me.

"Glad to meet you, Cos." I turned to Mary. "I'm sorry, but I have to tell you something upsetting."

Mary sat down on the couch, Jude and Cos in

back of her, as though for protection. "It's about the needlepoint, right? It isn't old and fantastically valuable?"

"What did I tell you and Josh, Mary?" put in Jude. "Miracles don't happen."

"I don't know anything yet about the value of the needlepoint," I said.

"You wanted to talk about my family, and the history of my house. But I don't have much to tell you. Maybe we could go over there after Jude goes back to the salon."

"I'd like to do that," I agreed. "And you're right. That's why I called you yesterday. But this is something else." I hesitated. I had to tell her the truth, flat out. "Yesterday I took your embroidery and packet down to Lenore Pendleton's office for her to keep in her safe."

"Yes?" said Mary. "That's what you said you were going to do."

"But now everything's changed." I plunged forward. "This morning Rob and a friend of his found Lenore Pendleton's body, in her office. She'd been killed."

"Rob found her body? What was he doing in her office?" Mary asked. She seemed more interested in Rob's whereabouts than in Lenore's death. Or maybe the death hadn't sunk in yet.

"I don't know, Mary. I thought you might know. He told the police he was there to look at the needlepoint."

She shook her head. "That doesn't make sense. He didn't even like it. And he'd seen it Tuesday night."

"Have you talked to him today?" I asked.

"No. But that's not unusual. Most days he's out with Arvin until early afternoon." She started to put what I'd said together. "He and Arvin take the boat out between five and six in the morning. When was he at Mrs. Pendleton's office?"

"I don't know exactly," I admitted. "I assume it was about nine-thirty. That's when I saw the police cars heading toward her house."

"And he found her dead?" Mary looked confused. "Why wouldn't he have told me?"

"I don't know." I wanted to know that myself. "But he did the right thing. He called the police."

"'The police' is his brother. Of course he'd do that," said Mary. "When was Mrs. Pendleton killed?"

"Late last night or early this morning."

"I talked to her yesterday afternoon. She sounded fine then."

"You talked to her yesterday?"

"Around three. She told me you'd been by to drop off the embroidery. She'd just heard Rob and I were engaged."

I was the one who'd told Lenore that.

"She wanted to talk to me about all the things that would change, legally, if I got married."

"Really?"

"She asked a lot of questions about our plans. She was trying to tell me not to get married soon. I stopped listening after a while. It's my life. Rob and I love each other, and we're getting married. No one can tell me what to do after I'm eighteen."

I suspected Mary was right: Lenore hadn't seemed happy about finding out Mary was engaged. "Did you make an appointment to see her?"

"No. She was interrupted while we were talking. She got off the phone because someone came to her office. Just because she has fancy diplomas on her wall doesn't mean she knows what's best for me," said Mary defensively.

"True," I had to agree. "But now Lenore's gone. When she was found her safe was open. Your needlepoint was one of the things that was gone."

Mary looked at me. "The murderer stole my needlepoint?"

"And jewelry that was in the safe."

"Why would anyone take my needlepoint?"

"I don't know."

"And how would anyone know to look for it?" Mary looked dazed.

"I don't know, Mary. I have no idea. They may not have known what it was—just thought it might be valuable because it was in the safe."

To my surprise, Mary started crying. "I'm trying so hard. I hate going through everything Mom and Dad loved. Everything from when I was a little girl. Soon it's all going to be gone. I don't remember seeing the needlepoint before I found it in the attic. But it must have been important to someone in my family. I wanted to keep that little piece of my past." Tears were now running down her face. "Why would anyone take it? It was mine. Not anyone else's."

"Mary, it was just embroidery," said Jude, who looked confused about what was happening. "Rob said you were going to sell it anyway."

Mary shook her head rapidly. "No way. I was going to keep it."

I reached over and tried to hug Mary. Her body was stiff and unyielding. And now racked with sobs. "I didn't even want to show it to Rob," she said. "But he saw the leather packet and opened it. He took it to his mom's house, because she does needlepoint, and his brother said to take it to you. I didn't want to give it to anyone. It was mine. And now"—she sniffed— "it's gone. Lost forever."

"Maybe not forever," I tried to console her. "Ethan and Pete will figure out who murdered Lenore and find your needlepoint." I certainly hoped that would happen. But I had no way of knowing.

"It's not fair! Nothing important stays," she said again, shaking her head as the tears continued to flow.

That's when I knew Mary wasn't just talking about her needlepoint.

Chapter 14

Next unto God, Dear Parents I address
Myself to you in humble thankfulness.
For all care and Pains on me bestowed and
The means of learning unto me allowed.

—Stitched by Eliza Hills, age twelve, at the
   Pinkerton Academy in Londonderry,
   New Hampshire, 1820

Jude left to go back to Maine Waves, Cos
promised to clean up the kitchen, and a few
minutes later, calmer, Mary seemed to pull herself together. "You wanted to see my house. Why
don't we go now?"

I agreed. Yes, I wanted to see her house. But,
even more, I didn't think she should be alone.
She was more upset about the loss of the needlepoint than I'd thought she'd be.

Its loss was one more in a life that had already suffered too many.

I understood that.

Mary's house looked the way I'd imagined a house built in 1770 would: two stories with a center door, white clapboard with green shutters, and a large chimney in the center of the pitched roof. Homes built then were heated by fireplaces; a house that size must originally have had at least five, all on the inner walls of the house, their chimneys joining at the roof. To help keep rooms warm, second-floor ceilings were lower than those on the first floor.

She unlocked the front door. "I was working here this morning. Mom always left the door unlocked during the day, but I don't like leaving it open when I leave."

"I understand. I lock my house when I leave, too," I assured her. "It's safer that way. You need to take care of yourself." Lenore Pendleton had trusted people. She'd opened her door to someone who'd killed her.

She shrugged. "Cos says I'm scared about nothing. She and her parents never lock their doors, and I've lived with them two years now. No one they don't know ever comes in. Although . . ." She smiled a little. "Jude does sneak out at night. It's easy when the house is wide open."

I wondered if Mary snuck out at night, too.

"Does Jude have a steady boyfriend?"

Mary hesitated, as though she wasn't sure if she should say. "Since Josh Winslow came back to town last spring, she's been with him. I don't know how serious he is, but she's ready for a ring." She glanced down proudly at her own small diamond.

"Josh doesn't even have a steady job," I blurted.

"She knows that. But Jude's doing well at Maine Waves. She says Josh hasn't had the right chance to show what a good worker he is."

I remembered Ob and Anna talking about all the jobs Josh had lost. He'd settle in for a couple of months and then get restless and bored. Employers would only be patient for so long. Didn't sound like Josh had proved he could settle down enough to be good husband material.

"I keep telling her Josh isn't as dependable as my Rob. And to think of what Arvin's poor wife, Alice, is going through!"

"I don't know her," I said. "Are they having problems?"

"Sure are. They got married a year ago, and then Alice got pregnant, practically on their honeymoon. Arvin had his own business, although he's still paying off that lobster boat of his. But he leaves Alice at home alone all the time, and hardly gives her enough money for groceries. They have a cute little boy, but Arvin says he can't stand the baby's crying." Mary looked at me. "Alice does all she can, cooking Arvin's favorite foods, and trying to keep the baby quiet. But she's afraid one day he won't come home, and she'll be left alone with the baby. I told Jude to think about Alice when she's dreaming about marrying Josh."

I'd just been filled in on the Haven Harbor gossip column. I didn't even know Alice Fraser, but I felt sorry for her. Young and in love was one thing. Young with a baby and an unsympathetic husband was another.

I changed the subject. "You don't live far from me. I hadn't realized this was your house."

"Yup. This is it. I'm afraid the place is in the stage my mom used to call 'worse before better.'"

I had to agree. The living room floor was covered with boxes of all shapes and sizes, both full and empty.

"I'm trying to sort everything in the house and barn. Some cartons are for things I want to keep. Some are for Goodwill. Some are to throw out. And some are things that may be worth selling. Rob's already called a couple of auctioneers to come and take a look at those cartons and the furniture."

"You're doing this by yourself?" I asked. I walked around the room, peeking into the uncovered boxes. Books, linens, china, kitchen miscellanea. One carton of board games and jigsaw puzzles. One of tools.

Another dozen or two were closed.

Mary nodded. "Most of the time. Cos comes with me some days, but she gets bored pretty fast. I've been working on the house for months, after school and weekends. Now that it's summer vacation, I'm here every day. Every time I think I have it under control I find another drawer or wardrobe or trunk to sort through. I've been going through the attic for the past couple of weeks. That's where I found the needlepoint. The realtor says I have to clear everything out except a few pieces of furniture before he puts the house on the market. I've got a lot of work to do before September."

Gram always said, "Use it up, wear it out; make do, or do without." That philosophy explained why Mary's house, and mine, were so full of the things previous generations thought "too good to throw out." Recycling wasn't a new concept in New England.

"Why don't you and Rob move in here?" I asked, looking around. "It's a beautiful house. You have more than enough furnishings to start out with. You could discard what you didn't want."

"That's what I wanted to do," Mary answered, clearing a space on the couch where we could sit. "But Rob said we should begin our marriage with everything new. That he wouldn't feel comfortable living in the house I'd grown up in. Plus, of course, he's hoping we get enough money from the sale of the house for at least a down payment on a lobster boat." She tucked a loose strand of hair behind her ear.

"Just make sure you're doing the right thing for yourself, Mary," I said.

"What's right for Rob is right for me. He's going to be my husband." She looked down proudly at the ring on her left hand.

"It's your life, too," I blurted.

"Yes. It's my life. And I've made my decision."

"Mary," I said softly, before she started crying again. "What do you know about your family's history? About the people who lived in this house."

"Since I saw you the other night I've been

thinking about that." she said, sniffing and wiping her eyes with tissues again. "Before you asked me, I hadn't thought about it." She looked away from me, toward the stacks of boxes filling the room. "I didn't want to think about it."

"But you've thought about it since then," I encouraged her.

"I only remember one story. I told you, most of the men in my family were sea captains, all the way back to the man who had this house built."

"It's a beautiful, large house. A captain, especially if he owned all or part of his ship, would've been able to afford it."

"When I was a little girl, six or seven, my grandmother, my father's mother, told me stories about the people who'd lived here. My mother wasn't interested; she said all those people were dead and gone and didn't have anything to do with our lives today." Mary sniffed again and blew her nose. "I wish I remembered more of what my grandmother told me."

"What do you remember?"

"You said maybe the embroidery was done by Mary, Queen of Scots. None of the stories have to do with her. But one story was about another queen—Marie Antoinette."

My history was hazy. "The 'let them eat cake' queen?"

"That's the one. I remembered her name last night and looked her up on the Internet."

It didn't matter if you learned history in school today. The Internet would explain it.

"Marie Antoinette was a queen of France. My

grandmother told me a man from Boston, James Swan, lived in France when she was queen. He knew a lot of people there. Powerful, rich, people. He also knew Captain Stephen Clough, who lived here, because they'd fought together during the American Revolution."

I listened carefully.

"The captain was in the salt and spar trade."

I nodded. In colonial times tall, straight white pines in Maine, which made perfect masts and spars, were cut down and taken to England and traded for salt, essential for preserving food for winter. After the American Revolution the masts were traded to other European countries for salt and for fine goods not then produced in North America, like fabrics and perfumes and books and window glass.

"Anyway, this Boston guy wanted to help his friends in France. He knew people like Talleyrand and Lafayette. He asked my ancestor to take a load of masts for the French navy to France, and gave him letters to important people there, volunteering the captain's ship to help them escape to America." She paused. "One person he was trying to get out of France was the queen, Marie Antoinette, but she was in prison by the time he docked in Le Havre. The plot to rescue her failed. And every day it got more dangerous in France for people who had money. People who supported the king and queen were dragged from their homes in the middle of the night, everything they owned was stolen or destroyed, and their heads were cut off."

"They were guillotined," I said, remembering the part of that history I'd found most interesting. The violence and gore. No wonder I'd gone to work for a private investigator in Arizona.

"Right. So Captain Clough wasn't able to save the queen, or the other people he was trying to help. They were captured, and he sailed without them."

"Wow, cool story," I said.

Mary smiled. "All that fancy clothing and furniture and ornaments Captain Clough had in his ship went to Boston." She gestured to the stacks of boxes filling her living room. "If any of it came to this house, it's been gone a long while."

"I'm glad you remembered the story," I told her. "Even if it has nothing to do with the embroidery."

"Any needlepoint on that ship would have been French, wouldn't it?" she asked.

"I would think so," I agreed.

"I remember my grandmother saying the captain didn't tell anyone but his wife about his adventure, because it was only a few years after our own revolution. People in Haven Harbor were cheering for those in France who were revolting—not for the king or queen."

"That makes sense."

"One other thing my grandmother said stuck in my mind. She said to remember that I was special, because I was a Mary, like all those other Marys."

"What did she mean by that?" I asked. "'All those other Marys'?"

"I don't know," said Mary. "When she said that, I thought it was a made-up story. I wish I'd asked more questions when she was alive. Now she's gone, and my parents are gone. All I have left are cartons of their stuff."

"That's not all you have," I reminded her. "You have one of their stories. And, whether or not we can get your needlework back, I'm going to try to find out more of those stories. They're yours, and one day they'll be your children's."

"Thank you," said Mary. Her eyes were dry, and her voice was soft but firm. "Thank you for understanding. No one else seems to."

I reached over to hug her. This time she hugged me back.

Chapter 15

Happy the woman who can find
Constant resources in her mind
She for amusement need not roam
Her pleasure centres in her home
And when the spring of life is o'er
She still enjoys the sacred store
Which youth should seek and value most
And when once gain'd can ne'er be lost.

—Stitched by thirteen-year-old
Susan Gray, in Boston, 1803

Mary was being more understanding about the loss of her needlepoint than I'd expected. But I was determined to get it back for her. It symbolized her family. She shouldn't have to lose any more than she already had.

On my walk home I called Sarah and Ruth and Nicole and left messages.

I kept wondering why Rob had gone to Lenore Pendleton's office to see the needlepoint. He'd already seen it. And he hadn't seemed interested in anything but its value. But then, Pete and Ethan had said he was with a friend.

Arvin Fraser and Josh Winslow were the only two friends I'd seen him with recently, and I couldn't imagine either of them being even remotely interested in needlepoint.

Jude and Cos had seen the needlepoint, since Mary lived with their family.

Of the three young men, Josh was certainly most familiar with embroidery. His dad was a Mainely Needlepointer, and Gram was teaching his mom to stitch. But I couldn't imagine Josh with a needle.

I called Pete Lambert.

He answered immediately. "Angie. Did you remember anything else about your meeting with Lenore Pendleton that might help us?"

"No. Sorry, Pete." The cell connection wasn't strong. Pete's voice was almost drowned out by a chorus of "dee! dee!"s from several chickadees who seemed to be following me down the street. Maybe I was near a nest. "I wondered . . . you said Rob Trask and a friend discovered Lenore's body. Who was with him?"

Pete hesitated. "Now, you're not going to get involved with this case, are you, Angie?"

"Of course not," I answered. I didn't tell him my fingers were crossed. "But I was just with Mary Clough, and she's very upset about her needlepoint being stolen. I'm wondering if you'd found out who was interested in it."

"We're doing our best to recover Mary's needlepoint and the missing jewelry. But our focus is on finding Lenore's killer."

"Right. But I assume one will lead to the other."

"Likely. But the killer could have broken up the jewelry so it couldn't be identified, and the stones might have been sold several times by now. I don't know why he or she took the needlework."

"It might be valuable."

"But you don't know that for sure. Whoever killed Lenore probably thought more jewelry was in that padded envelope and just grabbed it. If that happened, he could have dumped it when he saw what it was."

I winced. "I hope not. But I hope finding what was stolen will lead to the killer."

"And vice versa," Pete agreed. "Okay. I don't see any harm in telling you. Rob was with a young woman from Boston. Hold on a minute. I'll get you her name."

I heard the sound of papers being shuffled. I'd seen Pete's office. The Haven Harbor Police Department was not a paperless operation.

"Here; I found it. Her name's Uma Patel."

"An old friend of Rob's?" I was fishing, but I wanted to know more about this woman he'd taken to see the embroidery. And why.

"I don't think so. She's vacationing here. Staying at the Wild Rose Inn for a couple of days. I had a feeling she and Rob had just met. I don't think their relationship had anything to do with the robbery or murder, so I didn't press it. Do you recognize her name?"

"No; I've never heard it. I was just wondering."

"Don't wonder too many things, Angie. Ethan has this in hand. Right now we're asking people who live near Lenore Pendleton's office whether they saw anything suspicious. We're waiting for the ME's report to see when he thinks Lenore died. That should narrow our window down a lot."

"I understand. But thank you for sharing the woman's name," I said, clicking my phone off.

By the time I'd finished talking with Pete I was back at my house. I sat on one of the porch chairs and thought through everything that had happened.

If Rob had just met this Uma Patel, why had he taken her to see the needlepoint? He was engaged, so I hoped the answer wasn't that he was trying to impress her.

But then, he'd been at the Harbor Haunts Café a couple of nights ago without Mary. Sarah had seen a young woman with the lobstermen there. And that same girl had been with them the next night, at the co-op. Could that have been Uma Patel? I didn't know.

If she was a visitor from Massachusetts, as Pete had said, finding Lenore's body had certainly made her vacation memorable.

I'd put my phone on vibrate when I'd been talking with Mary. Now it was buzzing again.

It was Nicole Thibodeau, from the patisserie.

"Nicole! Thank you for getting back to me. Is Henri back yet? How is his mother?"

"His mother is not so well. He is staying another day or two. But I had time to look at that paper you left for me. The copy of the old note?"

"Yes. Could you read it?"

"With difficulty. I can't decipher who it seems to be addressed to. But the author thanks this person for her dear friendship and wishes her good health in the future. She is loved and remembered. It's signed 'Marie.'"

I'd been taking notes as fast as I could. "Nothing about Scotland or France?"

"No countries. It is written in French, of course. The words are faded, and the spelling isn't as it would be today, you understand."

"I do. Thank you for translating it."

"Not a problem. I wish I could have been of more help."

"You've helped a lot," I assured her. "We wanted to know what the note said, and you've told us."

What had I expected? That the note would say who'd made the needlepoint and how it had gotten to Maine?

That would have been nice, of course. Unlikely, but nice.

"Give my best to Henri. Tell him I'll be thinking of him and his mother."

"I will tell him. He is not being successful so far in finding a place for her to live." Nicole's voice dropped a bit. "He has been saying perhaps she should come to live with us."

"But you said she had Alzheimer's, and a stroke."

"*Oui.* It would not be easy for her, or for Henri and me if she were to come here. She needs so much attention. And we cannot afford to pay for a nursing home in this country, so if she comes here, it will be to us. It may have to be so."

What more was there to say?

Thank goodness Gram was healthy. Some days she seemed to have more energy than I did. And now she had Tom to help care for her if she should be ill. Since Tom was almost fifteen years younger than she was, chances were he'd still be around if she got sick.

I shook my head. I shouldn't even be thinking of such things. Gram and Tom were both fine, and likely to remain so for many years. I certainly hoped so.

Inside the house I gave Juno a few scratches behind her ears and checked to see that she had enough water. She was fine, despite her plaintive cries. I suspected she was just missing Gram.

I was, too.

I got a beer from the fridge. Late afternoon wasn't too early for a drink. Especially on a day someone had been murdered.

Sarah would return my call after her shop had closed. Maybe by then she would've had time to read more about medieval needlepoint. Had she heard about Lenore's death? Probably. Haven Harbor was a small town. If she hadn't, I'd tell her.

I'd left the front door open and the screen door latched.

I couldn't miss the footsteps on the porch and the repeated knocking on the door.

"Angie! Angie Curtis! Where've you been?"

I put down my drink and walked to the door. Rob Trask's face was flushed and I could smell the beer on his breath through the screen door. "Finally. You're home. I must have knocked on this door four times today!"

"What is it, Rob?"

"Lenore Pendleton, that lawyer who was going to help you? She's dead. Dead!"

"Your brother and Pete Lambert told me." He must have started drinking hours ago, but it wasn't every day he found a body.

That didn't mean I'd unlock the screen door. Drink affected people in different ways. "They told me you were the one who found her."

"This morning." Rob leaned on the door frame. His words were slurred.

"That must have been pretty awful." Especially for Lenore.

"It was." He paused for a moment, as though remembering. "Ethan says the needlepoint is gone. Gone! You promised to keep it safe."

"I know, Rob. And I'm sorry." Of course, if I'd known Lenore Pendleton was going to be killed and robbed I wouldn't have left the needlepoint in her care. "I'm sure your brother will find whoever killed her. I'm looking for the needlepoint, too. Mary's upset about losing it." When a woman was dead, it seemed bizarre to be worrying about an old piece of cloth no one even knew existed until a few days ago. But Rob was focused on losing something he thought of as his. Maybe that was his way of not thinking about Lenore's body. "I'll do my best to find it. For Mary."

"Right. Mary," said Rob. Had he told her about Lenore's death? He hadn't when I'd seen her, only a couple of hours before. I suspected he hadn't talked to her today.

"Who was the woman with you this morning, Rob?"

He looked at me a bit sidewise. "How'd you know anyone was with me?"

"Ethan and Pete Lambert told me."

"Oh, yeah. Her name's Uma something. Funny name, Uma. She was going to help Mary and me." He looked at me and stressed Mary's name. He'd understood I was emphasizing her loss. He might not have been as drunk as I'd first assumed. "Help Mary and me find a buyer for the needlepoint. She works at that fine arts museum down in Boston. She said people there would know how old the embroidery was, and if it was valuable. If it was important, whatever that meant, she said the museum might find a patron to buy it for their collection."

"How did Uma hear about the needlepoint to begin with?" The needlepoint I'd told Rob and Mary not to mention to anyone.

"I sort of told her. The guys and I were hanging out at Harbor Haunts, and she was at the bar by herself, and I just thought, her being an intern at a museum and all . . ."

"She's an intern? Not on the staff?"

"Interns are on the staff, aren't they? Anyway, that doesn't matter. She knows about all that old

material and stuff. I thought she could help
Mary and me." He glanced at me again. I had
the feeling he was making sure I'd heard the
name Mary again. "So I said I'd take her to see
the thing. No harm, no foul, right? Maybe she
could help you and Sarah figure out what it was."

"I see. So you and Uma went to see Lenore . . ."

"I figured it was important, and Uma's only in
town for a couple of days. Josh agreed to work
the boat for me today. And . . . you know what we
found."

At first Rob had looked angry. Now he just
looked disappointed. "We sure didn't think we'd
find a dead person."

"No."

"So, how long do you think it'll take for the
cops to figure out who killed that lawyer, and
where the needlepoint is?"

I shook my head. "Talk to your brother.
Ethan's the state trooper on the case. He'd know
more than I would."

"He's pretty busy. He went up to Hallowell to
get Emmie and bring her back here. They're
going to stay here so he can be in town for the
investigation, and Mom and Dad can take care
of Emmie. He doesn't talk a lot about his work,
especially with Emmie around."

Emmie was Ethan's three-year-old daughter,
and the center of his life while his wife was with
her National Guard unit in Afghanistan.

"But I need to know." He looked at me, a sad-
ness in his eyes that seemed more than the effect
of the beer. "That needlepoint was my chance. My

chance to stop living at home and being Arvin's sternman. To set up a business on my own."

"Your brother's a good detective," I assured him. "He'll find out what happened to the needlepoint."

And I'll be trying, too, I added to myself.

I understood, in a crass sort of way, why someone would murder for fine jewelry or cash. But needlepoint?

It didn't make sense.

No sense at all.

Chapter 16

Two celebrated Embroiderers whose works are found in almost every Collection [are] Mary Queen of Scots and Marie Antoinette, the wife of Louis XVI. To both these ill-fated ladies the Needle afforded a solace both before and during their misfortunes, as it has done throughout all ages to women who, though of not so exalted a rank, have yet had as many sorrows.

—Sophia Frances Anne Caulfeild and Blanche C. Saward, *The Dictionary of Needlework: An Encyclopedia of Artistic, Plain and Fancy Needlework*, 1882

After Rob left, Juno and I were alone in the quiet house.

I hoped Mary had gone back to the Currans. This wouldn't be a good night for her to be alone in her house.

What she'd remembered about the history of her family hadn't solved the mystery of who'd stitched the needlepoint and how it had gotten to Haven Harbor. I checked the computer to make sure: Mary, Queen of Scots, died in 1587 in England and Marie Antoinette died in France in 1793—more than two hundred years later. One site said Marie Antoinette had done needlepoint.

So both Mary and Marie—two women with different versions of the same name—had left the countries they'd been born in and become queens of France. Both had been imprisoned. Both had been beheaded. And both were needlepointers.

Interesting. But those facts wouldn't help me figure out where Mary's needlepoint was. I'd managed to entrust it to the only person in Haven Harbor who'd been murdered yesterday.

None of it made sense.

I scrambled myself two eggs, added a little cheddar and parsley—parsley was a vegetable, right?—and found a couple of blueberry muffins in Gram's freezer from last summer's crop. I'd have to ask Gram how she made her muffins if I wanted any this year. She'd soon be baking muffins for her husband, not her granddaughter.

What should I do next?

I paced the living room (which was also the Mainely Needlepoint office) while I tried to sort it out. So many questions to answer. . . . How old was the needlepoint? How had it gotten into

Mary Clough's attic? And, most important, who had it now and how could I get it back to Mary?

I couldn't do everything. But, after all, I was the director of Mainely Needlepoint. I could delegate.

I called Sarah and Ruth. Sarah'd heard about Lenore's death; according to her, everyone in town knew within an hour of Rob's calling the police. Ruth hadn't heard the news. She'd been at her home all day, writing. "Chastity Falls" hoped to get her next erotic novel up on the Internet later this week.

Both Sarah and Ruth agreed to meet at Ruth's house the next morning, before Sarah opened her shop, to talk about what we needed to do. I promised to bring croissants from the patisserie.

Then I called the Wild Rose Inn, where Uma Patel was staying, and left a message for her to call me back.

I realized I was on my second beer.

That wasn't going to help me think through what had to be done. Although it had relaxed me.

But people shouldn't drink alone, should they?

I decided to walk down to the Harbor Haunts to have one more beer. Just one.

The bar was quiet. Josh Winslow was the only person I knew there. Where was Jude? Despite what Mary had said, maybe they weren't a couple.

"Evening, Josh," I sat on the stool next to him. "A Gritty McDuff's," I said to the bartender.

Josh looked surprised to see me. "Hi, Angie."

"Where're your friends tonight?"

"Friends?"

I took a sip of my Gritty. Maine brews were one of the things I'd missed in Arizona. Not that I'd been a legal drinker when I'd been in Maine. But it had never been hard to get an older person to buy you a six-pack, especially if you shared the purchase. "Arvin and Rob. And Jude Curran."

"I don't keep track of where everyone in Haven Harbor is."

"I heard you went out with Arvin today."

"No secrets in this town. Rob called in sick or hungover, and Dad didn't have a full boat today, so he said I could go." He looked at me closely, as though I had a message written on my face. "You checking up on me?"

"I saw Rob earlier. He mentioned you'd been sternman today."

"Right."

"So you'd rather lobster than work on the charter."

He shrugged and drank again. "Taking rich folks out fishing every day's no fun. Some of them are okay. Others don't have a clue. Dad's always telling me to be nice. Set up their hooks. Help them pull the fish in. Scrub the head when they're seasick or drink too much beer. Clean their fish for them. I'm not their servant."

"So, what would you like to do?" I was curious. "What's your ideal job?"

"Not working for anyone. Be my own boss." I hoped Josh had a ride home. His words were beginning to slur. "No one to tell me what to do or not do. Be my own man."

"Good luck with that," I said.

"Don't worry about me. I've got plans. Big plans. I'd like one of those jobs where you sit in a fancy office and have a pretty girl bring your coffee and answer your calls." He grinned. "Then I could go on vacation and pay some other guy to clean the fish I'd caught and never get my hands dirty."

I finished my beer and put money on the bar. "I'm heading home."

Josh had already turned to talk to another woman at the bar.

I was beginning to feel those three beers.

Sounded as though Josh was getting restless again, just as Ob and Anna said he did. His ideal job had disappeared fifty years ago, if it ever existed. I had a feeling he wouldn't be sticking around town for long. Jude Curran might be disappointed if he left town, but I wondered if anyone else would miss him. In addition to his parents, of course.

Ob and Anna Winslow were good people. I hoped Josh would get his act together soon. For his parents' sake if not for his own.

It had been a long day. I took a hot shower and turned off my light about ten o'clock. I hadn't gone to bed that early since I was in junior high school and Gram had checked to make sure I got eight hours of sleep.

The night was dark, but I could hear cars and people in the street below my bedroom window.

Juno yawned and curled up at the bottom of my bed.

I tried not to think about Lenore Pendleton. Had she been killed for the jewelry in her safe, or was there another reason someone wanted her dead?

Tomorrow I'd check with Glenda, her secretary, and see if she'd discovered any of Lenore's files missing, or anything else out of place in her office. No one had told me not to talk to Glenda. And Uma. I hoped she hadn't gone back to Boston. I wanted to talk to her, too.

The next thing I knew Juno was kneading my shoulder.

I opened my eyes. Had I really slept until six in the morning?

By six-thirty I was at the patisserie. During the summer Henri and Nicole opened early. Nicole opened the door. "*Bonjour*, Angie! You're up early."

"You're up early every day."

Nicole shrugged. "Baker's hours. I've been here since four. But I get to sleep early."

I didn't volunteer that I'd gotten to sleep early the night before. Six-thirty still seemed too early for me. "Thank you again for translating the note," I said.

"You're welcome. I wish I could have been more help. I tried to read the name of the person it was addressed to. It says 'Ma chère' . . . but the name is blurred. Last night I looked again at the copy you left for me, and even used a magnifying glass. If I had to guess I would say the name begins with an *S*, but it is *très difficile* to decipher. Very hard." She shook her head. "Did you hear about poor Mrs. Pendleton? Killed in her own office."

"I heard. Very sad."

"I hope the police find the person who did that. Until then it is hard to feel safe. When Henri and I moved to Haven Harbor we thought we had left crime behind in Quebec." She sighed. "Now, not so much."

I nodded. I hoped I looked more confident than I felt. "In the meantime, could I have three of your croissants?"

"Of course, of course," she said, moving to the case where the day's baked goods and pastries were displayed.

"And three almond-cinnamon buns," I added. Starting the day with sugar would be good. "Is Henri home yet?"

"Later today, he'll be here. He left Quebec early this morning," Nicole said, ringing up my purchase. I handed her a twenty-dollar bill.

"How is his mother?"

She shrugged. "A little better. He'll tell me more when he gets home. For now, she's staying in Canada. We will be looking for a place for her here," she added. "And looking for the money we'll need to take care of her."

I took the white box she'd tied with a string and headed up the hill to Ruth's house. She lived next to the church, not far from anywhere in downtown Haven Harbor, but a distance she was having more trouble navigating every month. Arthritis wasn't fatal. But it wasn't kind.

She answered the door right away. She'd been waiting for me.

"Coffee's hot," she said, looking at the box I was carrying. "And I see you've brought treats. What fun! Plates are in the cabinet next to the refrigerator. I left cups on the counter next to the coffee." Ruth walked slowly into her living room. She already had a cup of coffee on the table next to her usual chair.

"Your coffee smells wonderful!" I called back to her. "I'll bring the pastries into the living room."

I'd put them on her coffee table when the doorbell rang. I went to answer it so Ruth wouldn't have to get up again.

"Do I smell coffee?" Sarah asked as she walked in the door. "Good morning, Ruth."

"Ruth has coffee all ready in the kitchen." I held up my cup.

"Go on into the kitchen and help yourself," Ruth added.

Within a few minutes we were all in the living room. No one said anything for a few minutes as we devoured the pastries.

"These are almost worth getting up this early for," said Sarah, who'd finished her croissant and was starting on her cinnamon bun. "Now, explain exactly why we're here."

I put my cup down. "You both know about Mary Clough's needlepoint, and you know Lenore Pendleton was murdered. Yesterday I talked with Mary and Rob. Of course they're upset that the needlepoint's disappeared. Whoever killed Lenore stole the needlepoint and the jewelry that was in her safe."

"Strange that they took the needlepoint," Ruth pointed out. "Stealing jewelry makes sense. And the killer must have known it was there. I wouldn't think of a law office safe as a place to find jewelry. It's more likely to be kept in a home safe. Or a safe deposit box, if the jewelry is valuable."

"True," I said. "I hadn't thought of it that way. Ethan said most of the jewelry was Lenore's. Lenore's secretary is making a list of everything that's missing."

"I wouldn't think a family lawyer in Haven Harbor would have much jewelry," said Sarah. "Unless Lenore's family had money."

"Oh, she had plenty of money for a while," said Ruth. "Her husband, Charlie, used to buy jewelry for her when the stock market was doing well. And it did very well for quite a few years. I remember Lenore showing me a ruby ring he'd given her, all set with pearls. A big thing. What we called a cocktail ring back in the day." Ruth shook her head. "Few people dress for cocktails anymore, and Charlie certainly isn't buying Lenore jewelry now."

"Lenore said they were separated," I said.

"For at least a couple of years. Way I heard it, he fell apart when the stock market collapsed a few years back. His investments disappeared, and so did his bank account. He started drinking, too." Ruth shook her head and lowered her voice. "There were rumors he got nasty with Lenore."

"Then why aren't they divorced?" I asked.

"Only Lenore and Charlie know that for sure," said Ruth. "I heard he was looking for alimony. More alimony than she wanted to pay."

Sarah and I exchanged glances.

Interesting. But we were together for another

reason. "I'm sorry about Lenore's problems. But the reason I called you both is that Mainely Needlepoint has three jobs related to Mary's embroidery. We have to figure out how old that needlepoint is—or was. We have to come up with an educated guess as to how it got into the attic of Mary's house. And I told Mary and Rob I'd try to find it and bring it back to them."

Sarah shook her head. "Are you sure we should continue investigating the needlepoint when it's missing? Mary may never see it again."

"But you've already made a good start in finding out about its age. You both"—I looked from one of them to the other—"suggested that it looked Elizabethan. But I'd like you to keep reading those books you have, Sarah, and focus on figuring exactly what that needlepoint is."

Sarah nodded. "Okay. If you think we should keep working on that."

"Ruth, you started doing computer searches the other day and came up with Mary, Queen of Scots. Nicole, at the patisserie, tried to translate the note that was with the needlepoint. She says it's signed 'Maria,' and is addressed, she thinks, to someone whose name begins with an *S.* Here's her translation." I passed the paper on which I'd scribbled down what Nicole had said. "I talked with Mary yesterday. She told me her house may have a connection to Marie Antoinette."

"I remember that old story," said Ruth. "I always thought it was a legend. That a captain who lived in that house tried to help Marie

Antoinette escape from the Bastille, but failed. What has that got to do with the embroidery?"

"I don't know," I admitted. "But Mary Stuart and Marie Antoinette were both queens of France. The note Nicole translated for us is written in French. What I'd like you to do, if you have the time, is to see if there's any connection between those two queens that would explain the needlepoint."

"You're right that they were both queens of France," Ruth pointed out. "But two hundred years apart! Not exactly best friends."

"That's why it's going to take work to find the connection."

Sarah looked doubtful. "You're pushing it, Angie. You want to help Mary. But how could there possibly be a connection?"

"I don't know. But I want us to try to find one."

"And while I'm studying up on embroidery techniques and Ruth is making an impossible historical connection, what will you be doing?" asked Sarah.

"Me?" I smiled at my two friends. "I'm going to find out who took the needlepoint from Lenore's office so we can return it to Mary."

Chapter 17

Believe not each aspersing tongue
As most week persons do
But still believe the story wrong
Which ought not to be true.

—Sampler stitched by Ariadne Hackney
    in Mercer, Pennsylvania, 1817,
    in satin, flat, and cross-stitch; sprays
    of roses in each corner, verse in
    center

Having agreed to their assignments, Sarah headed back to her store and Ruth to her computer.

I decided to find the mysterious Uma.

The Wild Rose Inn, where Pete had said she was staying, and where I'd left a message the day before, was within walking distance. A long walk, but not far enough so I needed to go home and get my car. The sea air was still cool, although the sun was quickly burning lacy patterns of dew off the grasses. Dandelions had already gone to seed, but tall buttercups kept unmowed lawns yellow and hid forget-me-nots in the grasses below them.

Mainers could be house-proud, but lawn care for most people meant mowing once a week or as necessary. As long as the lawn was green, witchgrass and dandelions and crabgrass were, if not welcomed, at least not hunted down.

With few exceptions, gardening time was spent on practical vegetable gardens, or in encouraging perennials like the orange daylilies that were beginning to bloom along the sides of the road. The last of the lupines were dying down, preparing to bloom again next June.

I'd missed the greenness of Maine when I'd lived in Arizona, where the botanical garden displayed seemingly endless varieties of cacti, and homeowners surrounded their homes with rocks and stones in varying shades of tan.

A chipmunk scampered in front of me and dove through a small opening in a stone wall separating two properties. Walls here were low, made of stones dug from gardens and foundations. Walls in Arizona had separated homes as though those inside were hiding or needed protection.

The Wild Rose Inn was a large yellow Victorian, the kind of house that once was filled with children and laughter. Today, most houses like that were divided into apartments, or made into bed and breakfasts or inns, as this one had been.

Large old homes were hard to maintain and heat. Many inns closed after Columbus Day and didn't open again until April or May to avoid oil bills.

I rang the bell on the wide porch that surrounded two sides of the house. An empty coffee mug had been left on the arm of one of the wicker chairs. The hammock looked welcoming. Maybe I should get a hammock for my porch.

"Yes?" said the gray-haired woman wearing jeans and an apron who answered the door.

"I'm Angie Curtis. I live down on Elm Street," I explained. "I'm looking for Uma Patel. I was told she was staying here."

"Pleased to meet you, Angie," she said. "I'm Mrs. Clifford, new owner of the Wild Rose. Uma's inside, having breakfast. Why don't you come in?"

The dining table was set for eight. Fourth of July week, and the small inn was busy. A couple in their thirties, perhaps honeymooners, sat at one end of the table, focusing on each other and on a tourists' guide to Maine. The Nolins, the art dealers from Canada, were at a small table to the side. I slid into the chair next to the young woman with long black braided hair at the far end of the large table. "Uma? I'm Angie Curtis. I left a message for you last night."

"Would you like coffee?" Mrs. Clifford offered. "Or breakfast? It's all prepared."

"Just coffee, thank you. Black." If I hadn't been full of pastries I'd have been tempted by the cranberry bread and omelets she was serving.

Uma stared at me. "I don't know you," she said. "That's why I didn't return your call."

"Yesterday you and Rob Trask discovered Lenore Pendleton's body."

"Who told you that?" She kept her voice low. Maybe she hadn't shared that information with her hostess or the other guests. Luckily, they weren't paying attention to anyone but each other.

"Ethan Trask. The state trooper who's investigating Lenore's death. I've spoken with Rob, too."

"Are you an investigator?"

"Something like that. Rob told me you went to see Lenore Pendleton because you wanted to look at needlepoint he'd told you about."

"That's right. We had nothing to do with the murder."

"I understand that. But I wondered where you'd heard about the needlepoint."

"From Rob, of course. After the fireworks, on the Fourth. I met him at that little café downtown."

She was wearing long blue sea glass earrings. Probably a souvenir of her trip to Maine. Cobalt blue sea glass was one of the rarest kind; most the result of Milk of Magnesia bottles thrown away years ago, broken on rocks, and smoothed by waves and sand.

"The Harbor Haunts."

"That's it. Anyway, I was by myself. I'm here for a few days on vacation, just a quiet time away from the city." Uma rolled her eyes. Clearly finding a body hadn't been high on her list of things to do on her vacation.

"You're from Boston?"

"That's where I live now. I grew up in Connecticut. What does that matter to you?"

"So, you were at the bar having a quiet drink by yourself."

"I wasn't looking for company, you understand," she said a bit defensively.

She was twenty-four or -five. A little younger than I was. And she wasn't wearing any rings on her left hand.

On vacation by herself. But maybe she hadn't wanted to stay by herself.

Been there. Done that.

"So you met Rob at the café."

"He and his friends were there. After a few minutes one of them . . . Josh? The cute one with blond hair. He asked if he could buy me another drink. And I agreed. Why not?"

Why not, indeed?

"I started talking to them. They were different from people in Boston. They all lived here. I told them I was vacationing. They asked what it was like to live in a city. I said I hadn't lived there long; I was interning at the Museum of Fine Arts." She looked at me and explained, "I was an art history major in college. Jobs for people like me don't come easily."

"I understand," I said, although I didn't, really. Anyone with a college degree was in another world from that of most of the guys who lobstered. Or from me, who'd done office work for a PI until my boss was sure I could handle a camera and a gun. On-the-job training.

"So, you told them you were at the MFA."

"Right. And then Rob told me about this old piece of needlepoint he'd found."

He'd found, I noted. Interesting.

"He said it might be from Elizabethan times, and he was trying to find out exactly how old it was. He thought it might be worth a lot of money, and he didn't want to be cheated."

"Of course not," I said.

"I told him I'd look at it." Uma picked at her eggs with her fork, and then looked at me. "Honestly, I'm not an expert on Elizabethan textiles. But I thought if I saw it I might be able to tell him something about it. And if this guy's needlepoint was spectacular I might be able to get the museum interested. It would show my boss how serious I am about working there. Prove I could help with acquisitions."

"Which might lead to a permanent position there?" That wasn't hard to guess.

Uma nodded. "That's what I'm hoping for."

"But you never saw the needlepoint."

"We walked into the house, where the woman's office was . . . and there she was, lying on the floor, near her desk. Her head was bloody, and there was blood on the floor." Uma paled a little, remembering. "I'd never seen a body before. I left, fast, and went outside."

"What about the needlepoint?"

"We never saw it. I waited outside while Rob called the police, or the state troopers. I don't know. But whoever he called came fast. Rob's brother asked me a few questions, like who I was and why I was there, and what I'd seen. I told him what I'm telling you. Except the part about hoping the museum would offer me a real job, of course. I figured he wouldn't care about that. I overheard another policeman say the safe was open. I didn't see it. Rob told him about the needlepoint, and they said nothing like that was in the safe. Then they said I could go, so I did. I spent the afternoon at the beach, trying not to think about what I'd seen." Uma shuddered. "What an awful way for that woman to die. But I would have liked to have seen the needlepoint."

I nodded. "Have you heard from Rob since then?"

"No. But last night I did get a call from one of the other guys I met Tuesday. He's a lobsterman. He invited me to come out with him on his boat. I told him, sure. I'd like that. I don't know anything about lobstering."

That "other guy" I assumed was Arvin Fraser. He was the only one of that group who owned a lobster boat.

"So you're going?"

"This afternoon. He invited me to go this morning, but he was taking his boat out about five. Way too early for me. I'm on vacation! He said he'd take me out later today and haul a few traps to show me how it's done."

"Have fun," I said. "And if you think of anything else that might be helpful in finding that missing needlepoint, give me a call or text me." I handed her one of my Mainely Needlepoint cards.

She looked at it. "You're interested in needlepoint, too," she said. "Have you seen that needlework Rob was going to show me?"

"I have," I assured her. "It is special. But I don't know how old it is."

"If you find it, and you'd like an expert at the MFA to take a look at it, let me know," she said. She reached into the blue canvas bag next to her chair, pulled out a generic MFA business card, and wrote her name and telephone number on the back. Interns probably didn't rate personal business cards. "I'd still be interested in checking it out. Or getting it to people who'd know about it."

"Thank you," I said, pocketing the card. "I'll remember that."

Chapter 18

—Sampler stitched by Francis Wilcox,
age fourteen, in 1820. Includes four
alphabets, chain, eyelet, tent, and
stem stitch, with a vine border, four
rosettes in the corner, and two caskets.

It was a perfect day for a boat ride. The kind of
Maine day people traveled hundreds of miles to
enjoy.

I hoped Uma would have a fun afternoon
with Arvin. And I was glad to have her card. If—
when—the needlepoint was recovered, she might
be a good contact person. I had faith in the
Mainely Needlepointers. We could research and
figure out a lot about the embroidery. But we'd
need to contact experts before our conclusions
were definite.

I wondered for a moment whether I should
have mentioned to Uma that Arvin was married

and a father. But going lobstering wasn't exactly a romantic date.

Or maybe it didn't seem romantic to me because I'd grown up with the smell of bait.

Uma had a simple story: she was on vacation, and happened to be with Rob when he found Lenore's body. I believed her.

What kept bothering me was an obvious question I hadn't heard an answer to: why had anyone killed Lenore Pendleton?

Yes, the needlepoint and jewelry were missing. Since no one'd mentioned her safe's being broken into, I assumed she'd opened it for someone. Someone who'd threatened her? But she hadn't been shot or stabbed. She'd opened the door when she was wearing nightclothes. The murder weapon had been a marble bookend.

Some day in the past she'd bought those bookends, maybe at an antique show or auction. She couldn't know that one of them would be used to kill her.

Who would she open her front door—and her safe—for? A person she knew. But even if she'd opened her door, only a threat would make her open her safe.

She'd promised me she wouldn't give the needlepoint to anyone but Mary or me.

What if Rob had decided to get the needlepoint back? He'd been clear he wanted to sell it. What if Rob had killed Lenore to get it?

But, no. That didn't make sense, for so many reasons.

First, why would he have killed Lenore and then returned a few hours later with Uma? His second visit would explain any fingerprints he'd left in Lenore's office. But was Rob that sophisticated a criminal?

Rob rubbed me the wrong way. But was he a killer and thief?

I couldn't think so. Not without a lot more evidence.

So far, before Lenore's secretary checked for sure, it looked as though the thief and murderer hadn't taken any files. If that was true, it ruled out a frustrated or angry client. And if someone was angry at Lenore, and wanted to kill her, why would they bother to have her open her safe?

Whoever killed her wanted what was in that safe. That was the only scenario that made sense.

But had they been looking for the needlepoint? Only a few people had even known it existed. The missing jewelry, on the other hand, was probably worth a lot of money. More people might have known about it. And jewelry would be easier to dispose of than needlepoint.

Whoever killed Lenore must have done it for the jewelry. They hadn't brought a weapon—or at least hadn't used one—so they'd assumed Lenore would open the safe for them. Which she did. But then, maybe because they didn't want a witness to the theft, they'd picked up the bookend and hit Lenore. Multiple times.

I shuddered, imagining.

So who knew about the jewelry?

Glenda, Lenore's secretary, certainly knew. The police had asked her to make a list of the safe's contents, with descriptions.

No one had told me I couldn't talk with Glenda.

And I'd met her at Lenore's office, so it wouldn't be like calling Uma, whom I'd never met.

"Glenda? Angie Curtis. I'm so sorry about Lenore. I wondered . . . would you mind if I stopped in to see you? I understand you're making a list for the police of everything that was in the safe."

Glenda sounded surprised that I'd called. But she agreed to see me.

I decided to take her something. A condolence gift to a family member was usually a casserole or dessert you could heat up or freeze. What did you take to someone who'd just lost her boss—and her job? Gram would have known. But I wasn't going to disturb her honeymoon with a Haven Harbor etiquette question.

Flowers? Chocolates? I'd take both. Glenda was a middle-aged woman who always looked a bit frazzled. I'd seen a picture of a toddler on her desk. Working mothers didn't get enough flowers or candy. (Did anyone?)

Glenda lived about ten miles down Route 1. On the way I'd pass a garden center and gift shop.

Juno meowed plaintively as I picked up my keys. Then, giving up on convincing me to stay, she headed for one of her favorite seats, in the kitchen window overlooking the backyard bird feeders.

Although she admired birds and squirrels from her choice of comfy seats inside windows, Juno didn't seem to mind being served her dinner rather than having to catch it.

"Thanks for reminding," I told her. I put down my keys and filled all Gram's bird feeders.

It wouldn't do for her to come home and find empty seed and suet holders.

I'd be home in plenty of time to replenish Juno's food dish.

Glenda's home was a double-wide with a carport.

She answered the door wearing sweatpants and a pink T-shirt reading "#1 Mom" on it. "You came at a good time, Angie. Tyler's taking a nap." She led me through the toys on the floor to a seat in the living room. "I've already told the police I'd like to help. But I don't know a lot. Except"—she frowned—"that I'll be looking for a new job. And Lenore won't exactly be able to give me a recommendation."

I sympathized. But I needed information.

I handed her a bouquet of daisies and baby's breath, and a box of dark chocolates. "These are for you. You were close to Lenore. And I promise not to bother you for long."

"The flowers are lovely," she said. "I'll get a vase. And I'll hide the chocolates from my husband." She winked at me as she put the chocolates on top of a cabinet and came back a few minutes later with a vase, now full of the flowers, which she put on a high table, far from a toddler's fingers. "They're beautiful, Angie. You didn't have to bring all these things . . . but I'm glad you did. I've been sitting here thinking about Lenore. I still can't believe she's dead. Murdered." She paused. "I keep wondering what would have happened if I'd been in the office the day she was killed."

"She was in her nightgown and robe when

they found her," I said. "She answered the door late at night. I haven't heard a specific time of death. So, if that's true, then you wouldn't have been there anyway."

"True. But that doesn't stop me from thinking about what might have happened."

"What was Lenore like to work for?" I asked, trying to be casual, and changing the subject.

"She wasn't easy, but she was fair," Glenda said. "I've worked in her office almost four years. She was always understanding about giving me time off when Tyler was sick, or if I needed to be with my family. But she could be tough. She had some clients—especially those getting divorced— who got wicked nasty. They'd yell at each other and at her. I was embarrassed just to be in the next room. But she never lost her temper. She had a way of calming people down." Glenda leaned toward me. "Her clients ended up with pretty good deals, too."

"She told me she was getting divorced."

Glenda frowned. "Should have gotten one years ago, if you ask me. That Charlie of hers was a pain. He'd come to the office and ask for money, or insist on seeing her when she was with a client. I told her she should get an order of protection. But she never did. She said she could handle him." Glenda stopped and looked at me. "Do you think Charlie could have killed her?"

"I have no idea. I heard he was asking her for alimony."

Glenda looked around, as though she didn't want anyone to overhear. But there was no one there. "I shouldn't be saying this, but she was too easy on him. She said they used to be good together, but I never saw that. She worked hard—long hours—and she earned all the money in that family. She was going to keep the house and her office. The settlement they were working on gave him enough to get a house like this one, or an apartment, but not much more. Of course, he isn't working, and," she added confidentially, "he drank away a lot of the money she gave him."

I shook my head. "Was he ever violent?"

She hesitated. "I don't think he ever hurt her. But he sure yelled a lot. In the last month or so he'd been yelling about her jewelry."

"Her jewelry?" I asked. "You mean the jewelry she had in her safe? The jewelry that was stolen?"

Glenda nodded. "Funny, isn't it? He said he'd spent thousands of dollars on that jewelry, back when he was making lots of money. That was before I worked for her, so I can't say that for sure, but Charlie sure said it. Said it all the time. He said she should give him at least half of the jewelry. That she owed it to him."

"And now neither of them will have it," I said. Unless, of course, Charlie had killed her for it, I thought to myself.

"Strange, isn't it? How life works out."

"Have you finished the list the police wanted?"

"While Tyler's napping I've been listing what I remember." She glanced in the direction of what I assumed was her son's bedroom. "We didn't have a master list of everything she kept in the safe. It never seemed we'd need a list. All

I have is my memory. This morning I went over to the office and looked through the papers that were still there. I couldn't remember seeing any others. Now I'm trying to remember all Lenore's jewelry. The police let me look through a box of photos she had upstairs, and I picked out those showing her wearing jewelry. She loved big rings, so she had several of those. One diamond ring and one with rubies were spectacular. She didn't wear her good jewelry very often. She dressed so her clients and the judges wouldn't think she was making money off poor people. She had a long string of pearls, and a sapphire necklace and bracelet that Charlie gave her for an anniversary present. He must have spent a lot on those pieces. When he listed what he thought she should give back to him, he always included those. And sometimes she wore a large emerald ring she told me she'd inherited. She hadn't gotten all her jewelry from Charlie. I just have to sit down and try to remember it all."

"And someone else's jewelry was there, too?"

"The rest was Elsie Sawyer's. She died a couple of months ago and her estate hasn't been settled yet. Her daughters both wanted the same pieces of jewelry, so Lenore was holding them until the three of them met, next month. Those pieces will be easy to identify. There's a list of the pieces, with pictures, in Elsie's file." Glenda smiled wryly. "Maybe neither of her daughters will get their mother's jewelry after all."

"And a piece of needlepoint in a brown leather case is missing."

Glenda shook her head. "I don't know anything about that. The police asked me, because one of the people who found Lenore said he'd gone to her office to see the needlepoint. But she must have added that to her safe this week. I never saw it."

"Do you have the combination to her safe?" I asked.

"No, only she had it. She once told me she'd also left it in her safe deposit box at the bank, in case she died and someone needed to open the safe." Glenda looked at me sadly. "That won't be necessary now."

Chapter 19

Failing to discover anything new about Lenore's death, or about the current location of the needlepoint, I headed back to Haven Harbor.

Close to town I passed Aurora, the home actress Skye West and her son Patrick were fixing up. Painters were scraping the shingles, and a backhoe was digging what I assumed would be a basement for Patrick's new studio and home, near the site of the destroyed carriage house. Sarah'd once mentioned he'd been working with an architect from his hospital bed in Boston.

It didn't look as though the Wests were wasting any time in getting the construction started. Money made a major difference in expectations. And the Wests certainly had money.

I decided to stop and see Ob Winslow, Josh's dad, and the only Mainely Needlepointer I hadn't been in touch with in the past week. He'd been busy with his fishing charter. I took that as a sign his summer was going well.

But still, I should keep in touch. I was a little worried about Josh, too. He'd looked stressed last night at the Harbor Haunts, and every time I'd seen him recently he'd had a beer in his hand.

Of course, so had I. But that was different. I had a house and a small company. I wasn't dreaming of jobs that didn't exist.

The Winslows' barn doors were open. I peeked inside, but no one was there, so I headed past the ell to the main house.

Anna answered my knock. "Hi, Angie! Good to see you. Coffee?"

"Thanks, Anna. I could use another cup."

"Ob's not here," she added over her shoulder as she headed for the kitchen. "He and Josh have a full charter today. Beautiful weather and Fourth of July week—a good combination for fishing."

"That's great," I agreed, following her. "I suspected they were pretty busy since I haven't heard from Ob for a while. I thought I'd stop in and see how all of you were doing."

She nodded as she poured us each a mug of

coffee. "We were a little worried about finances in June, as Ob probably told you. Too many cool, rainy days. Several of his charters were canceled at the last minute. Frustrating."

We sat at their bright yellow kitchen table.

"How's your needlepoint coming?" I asked. Ob was the serious needlepointer in this family. Gram was teaching both Anna and I to stitch, but Anna was way ahead of me. I told myself it was because she didn't have to run a business. I also suspected she was working on it harder than I was.

"My striped bass pillow cover is coming along," she said. "When your grandmother gets back from her honeymoon I'm going to ask her advice about the stitches I should use on parts of it. It's going to be a birthday gift for Ob, so I only work on it when he's not home." She paused. "Doing needlepoint relaxes me. All the stiches are concise and neat and in order. Not like the rest of life."

"Gram should be back soon," I told her. "Tom wants time to prepare for Sunday services. I heard the minister who substituted for him last week wasn't up to Tom's standards." I felt a little guilty at not attending the service myself. I'd treated myself to sleeping in.

"Sounds as though they've kept in touch," Anna said. "I'm so glad Charlotte found the right person for her. Now, I hope you find someone. And I'm always on the lookout for a nice girl for Josh."

What about Jude Curran? She'd certainly indicated she was interested in Josh. But if Anna didn't know about that, I wasn't going to tell her. "Don't worry about me. I'm doing fine. And Josh is only—what? Twenty-three?" I knew he was younger than I was. "He's got lots of time to find the right girl."

"He's twenty-two. But I'm hoping he'll find a girl who'll settle him down a little. Encourage him to get a regular job. Helping his father on the *Anna Mae* isn't anything permanent. And it would be nice if he could afford a place of his own. I love the boy, but he's too old to be living at home with Ob and me."

I nodded. "But at least he has friends in town. Sarah and I saw him the other night at the co-op with Arvin Fraser and Rob Trask." And Jude Curran and another girl.

She sighed. "Can't say that surprises me. Josh may be living here, but he doesn't spend much time with Ob and me. He works for Arvin whenever Rob can't and Ob doesn't need him. I worry about him spending so much time with Arvin and Rob. They were all close friends when they were in school. Peas in a pod, you'd think. Now Arvin drinks too much, if you ask me. I hoped he'd settle down after he got married last year, but Josh says the baby's crying gets on Arvin's nerves. I suspect he's finding excuses to stay away from home." She shook her head. "Not a good role model for Josh. And Arvin's poor wife, stuck at home with the baby while those boys hang out, as they say. Josh doesn't tell me much, of course. I'm just his mother. But so far as I can tell, the three of 'em don't do much 'cept drink beer and look for pretty girls."

"Maybe he'll fall in love with one of those pretty girls," I said, thinking of Jude.

"I suppose so. But it hasn't happened yet." So I was right. He hadn't mentioned Jude to his parents. Not a good sign for her. Although sometimes the parents were the last to know.

We sat and sipped our coffee.

"Sad news, Lenore Pendleton being murdered," said Anna. "I told Josh, you've got to be careful, even when you're in Haven Harbor. Wicked folks are everywhere."

I nodded. "You're right. Rob Trask and a tourist the guys met at the Harbor Haunts were the ones who found Lenore's body."

Anna put down her cup. "I heard Lenore was killed, of course. I didn't know any of Josh's friends were involved."

"I'm not saying they were involved in her murder. But Rob found her."

"Horrible."

"And whoever killed her stole jewelry from her safe, and a piece of needlepoint Sarah Byrne and I were trying to identify and left with her for safekeeping."

"You're trying to find Lenore's murderer?" Anna looked at me askance.

"Not her murderer," I corrected Anna. "The needlepoint that was stolen."

"You take care of yourself, Angie," Anna said. "Don't get yourself involved in another murder investigation. You'll never find a man that way. And look for a man who doesn't work on the water. I can tell you, being married to a man who takes his boat out several miles from shore almost every day isn't easy. You don't want a future sittin' and wondering if your husband will come home."

I didn't want a future just sitting anywhere.

It had been an exhausting day. I was glad to pull into my driveway. I was looking forward to a quiet evening. I hadn't planned anything, and I didn't expect Sarah or Ruth to have discovered any solutions to our needlepoint mystery during the afternoon.

I hadn't either. Uma hadn't known anything that brought me closer to finding the missing needlepoint—or the killer. And Glenda had confirmed what I'd heard other places: Lenore was in the middle of a contentious divorce.

I opened a can of beer, went to my computer, and idly ran local searches. Lenore's death was, of course, in all the local and state papers, but none of the articles included details I didn't already know. Out of curiosity, I Googled her husband. Charles Pendleton had a few traffic violations and one drunk and disorderly conviction. But what was most interesting was a picture of Lenore and Charlie in happier times.

Dressier times, too. The picture had been taken with artist Jamie Wyeth at a formal benefit for the Farnsworth Museum several years ago. Lenore was wearing a cocktail dress and a striking necklace. Was it the sapphire necklace Glenda had mentioned? The picture was black and white. I couldn't tell.

I stared at the picture.

Lenore and Charlie were both smiling. I didn't see any hint of trouble in their relationship.

Lenore hadn't changed much, although her hair was now a little more gray.

But I kept looking at Charlie. I was almost positive Charlie Pendleton was the man I'd seen leaving his wife's office the morning I brought her the needlepoint. The man who'd looked angry and who'd rushed off.

I sat back, trying to decide whether or not that was important. Glenda had said Charlie'd been bothering Lenore. Was that morning one of those times? Lenore had certainly been alive when he'd left her office that morning. Could he have returned later? Could Charlie have killed her? Perhaps he hadn't planned to—that bookend she'd been hit with was definitely a weapon of convenience, not premeditation. But, maybe . . .

On the other hand, the police had probably already talked to him. After all, since their divorce wasn't final, he was still Lenore's next of kin. I made a note of his address. I'd pay a sympathy call on the new widower tomorrow. I hadn't heard they'd had any children. Unless she'd made out a new will, he'd inherit her estate.

But she believed in having up-to-date wills. She'd talked to me about them several times. She'd probably changed hers when she and Charlie separated.

Had he known that?

My mind went back and forth, considering the possibilities.

I cooked a hamburger for dinner and then glanced through my embroidery books, but I couldn't focus on them.

Murder today seemed so much more important than embroidery four hundred years ago.

I thought of Mary, who'd frozen the first time I tried to hug her. Of Lenore, supporting herself and divorcing Charlie.

Had Lenore ever felt isolated? Had she ever lain in bed alone, longing for someone to touch her? I wondered.

When was the last time anyone hugged me, other than Gram? Her hugs were fine, but they weren't the kind I was thinking of.

When was the last time someone held my hand?

Sometimes I felt as though without a caring touch I'd crack and break into tiny pieces.

Sometimes I didn't even care if the touch was a caring one.

I poured a little brandy and took it up to bed with me.

I had to learn to live alone. I was strong. I didn't need to lean on anyone.

I fell asleep holding my pillow.

Chapter 20

Home, 'tis the name of all that sweetens life
It speaks the warm affections of a wife.
Oh! 'Tis a word of more than magic spell
Whose sacred power the wanderer can tell.

—Sampler stitched by Martha Agnes
Ramsay, age twenty-three,
Hopewell, Ohio, 1849

I woke in the dark.

Footsteps. Someone was in my house.

I rolled over and looked at the clock next to my bed. Eleven-thirty. I must have fallen asleep immediately.

Had I locked the doors before I'd come upstairs?

I was sure I had.

I heard the low murmur of conversation. More than one person was in the house. Downstairs.

Where my gun was. Why hadn't I brought my gun upstairs? Next time . . .

If there was a next time.

Juno jumped up from the foot of my bed, where she'd been snoozing, and went to investigate.

If I hadn't been so scared, I'd have laughed. An attack cat?

If I ever got a pet, it would be a dog. A big dog with a loud bark and sharp teeth.

I sat up slowly. I didn't turn my lamp on.

What was there to steal downstairs? I loved this house and its contents, but it wasn't full of valuables. Gram's silver was in the dining room, though. And my computer was new.

What had Lenore thought? Had she opened the door to her killer, or had she woken, as I just did, hearing someone downstairs in her office?

Maybe she'd been brave enough to go down and confront them.

But she'd died.

I'd always thought I was pretty brave. Now my heart was pumping so hard I could hear it. I felt frozen.

If only I had my gun.

Maybe whoever was in the house would take what they were looking for and leave. Maybe they'd think I'd sleep through a home invasion. My car was in the driveway; they'd know I was home.

My mind whirred.

Without thinking, I touched my angel necklace.

Then I heard footsteps on the stairs. The

fourth step from the bottom creaked, as it always had.

Should I pretend to be asleep? Should I confront whoever it was? What if whoever was on the stairs had a gun?

For a moment I was distracted by the sound of the downstairs toilet flushing.

So. One in the bathroom; one on the stairs.

I'd never thought of a burglar stopping to pee.

Then whoever was there knocked on my door. I'd left it ajar by habit.

"Angie? Angie, are you asleep? Angie, this is Tom. Your grandmother and I are back from Quebec."

Chapter 21

Full well she knows that winter keen
Must come to blast this painted scene.
With famine on its wing
Her prudent labours find repose
Not winter cold nor want she knows
Till time renews the spring.

> —Sampler by Mary Elizabeth Fearson,
> Georgetown, Washington, DC,
> circa 1834

I took a deep breath and reached to turn on my lamp.

"Tom!"

"I hope I didn't scare you. Before we go to the rectory Charlotte wanted to pick up the clothes she left here."

I pulled my terry cloth robe over my black

sleep shirt that read, "This is my sexy nightgown," and went to the door. "Why didn't you call?"

Tom stood in the hall, caught somewhere between embarrassed and amused when he saw me. "We thought we'd be home hours ago, but we stopped for dinner in Skowhegan and ran into a guy I'd gone to seminary with. Time flew. Your Gram's downstairs. She said she'd left suitcases in her room?"

"They're still there," I said, turning on lights in the hall and in Gram's room. Gram had been superstitious. She hadn't moved any of her things into the rectory before her wedding. But she'd packed most of her clothes in several suitcases and garment bags and left them in her room, ready to go. "How was the trip?"

"Wonderful," he said. "Perfect. Charlotte wants to tell you all about it. Why don't you go downstairs? She's in the kitchen. We smuggled some Quebecois cheeses and wine in for you. She wanted to put them away."

That was my Gram. I grabbed one of her filled suitcases and headed for the stairs.

Gram was home!

I felt as though I was seven and it was Christmas morning.

"Gram!" I grabbed her and gave her a big hug. "You and Tom practically gave me a heart attack! But I'm glad you're back. I want to hear all about your honeymoon—well, almost all!" I teased her. "And I have so much to tell you."

"We had a great time, Angel. Took lots of pictures and brought back lots of memories," she said. She looked great. Happy and calm. Juno was purring loudly and rubbing against her legs.

I hoped I looked as good as Gram when I was sixty-five.

"Tom told me you smuggled food over the border," I said.

"To thank you for your help with the wedding, and because you happen to be our favorite granddaughter." She pointed at two bottles of wine on the table and handed me a bag of wrapped cheeses.

"Of course, I'm your only granddaughter," I said, peeking into the bag. "Shall we sample these now?"

"No, they're all for you. We got some for ourselves, too. I hope we've written on each package what's inside."

"If not, then it will be a surprise."

"I kept thinking of Henri and Nicole's breads. They'd be delicious with the cheeses."

"And the wines," I said, looking over what she'd brought. I wasn't an expert on wines or cheeses, but I looked forward to learning.

The front door closed a couple of times.

"Tom's taking my suitcases out to the car. I'll come back tomorrow to get a few other things," said Gram. "It's late; close to midnight. We can get caught up in the morning."

I nodded. I wished she were staying here, in her old room. I wished we could sit up and talk the way we had when I'd been a teenager. I needed to tell her what had happened in Haven Harbor during the past few days.

The rectory was two blocks away. Two long blocks.

"Tom has to catch up with paperwork and get his sermon ready for Sunday, so I'll have plenty of time to catch up with you," she said, giving me another hug. "I'll see you in the morning, okay? And I'll take Juno home with me then," she added, reaching down to scratch Juno's neck. "One more day, my Juno, and you'll go to your new home."

We walked together toward the front door and I hugged her again before she left.

Then I was careful to lock both the screen door and the front door. And take my gun upstairs with me.

Gram was back.

And gone.

The house seemed emptier than ever without her.

Not that I'd ever admit that.

Chapter 22

The Quene his Majesties Mother wrote a book of verses in French of the Institution of a Prince, all with her own hand, wrought a cover of it with a needle, and it is now of his Majestie esteemed as a precious jewel.

—Written in 1616 by Bishop Montagu of Winchester about the book *Tetrasticha, ou Quatrains a son fils,* written in 1579 by Mary, Queen of Scots, for her son, James, while she was imprisoned. Today the book's whereabouts are unknown.

Gram hadn't come over first thing the next morning. I texted her and she said she'd see me around eleven. Could we have lunch together? I agreed.

I pulled myself together and decided to visit Charlie Pendleton.

For this condolence call I didn't take flowers or chocolate.

Charlie's current residence was the third-floor apartment in a rambling, unkempt farmhouse out on Route 1. Several cars and trucks were parked in the wide driveway and on the lawn. The beige sedan reminded me of the one Charlie had taken off in when I'd seen him at Lenore's office. Good. I hoped that meant he was home. The house needed a coat of paint and probably a new roof. Sarah would have called it vintage. I wondered if it had dependable plumbing and heat.

Four doorbells and four mailboxes were by the front door.

I pressed the button labeled "C. Pendleton."

I pressed it again.

The third time I leaned on it.

A few minutes later Charlie appeared at the door barely dressed in striped boxer shorts and a T-shirt. Neither of them covered his belly. I tried not to look at anything but his face.

He must have slept in this morning. He didn't look like a man in mourning for his murdered wife, unless the mourning had involved a lot of late night drinking.

I made an immediate decision to only talk to him at the door. I wasn't crazy enough to climb three flights of stairs to talk to a half-naked man known to have a temper.

"Yeah?" he asked. "Who're you? I got nothing to say to the press."

I couldn't match this man to the elegantly dressed gentleman I'd seen in the picture taken at the Farnsworth benefit a few years ago. Or to anyone I would have imagined Lenore Pendleton would marry.

"I'm not the press," I said. "I'm trying to find out what happened to the things taken from your wife's office safe the day she was killed."

I came right to the point. I didn't think Charlie was going to offer me coffee and doughnuts.

"You mean that jewelry I spent a fortune on?"

"And a piece of needlepoint that belonged to a client of mine," I said.

"Needlepoint?" he looked dubious.

"It was in a padded envelope." I wasn't going to explain any more than I had to. The fewer people who knew that needlepoint might be valuable the better.

"I don't know anything about any needlepoint," he said. "And, in case you're wondering, no, I didn't kill my wife. And, no, I don't have anything that was in that safe. I saw her the morning after the Fourth about some personal matters. We disagreed, as usual, because she's a b . . ." He didn't finish the word. I got the point.

"Did you know the combination to her safe?"

"No way she'd let anyone know that, even her own husband. She had private stuff in there from her clients, as well as jewelry that was rightfully mine."

I suddenly wondered how many people Charlie had told about that valuable jewelry in Lenore's safe. "Did you tell anyone about the jewelry?"

"Sure. Ain't no secret."

"Did anyone show a special interest in it? Or how valuable it was?"

"Missy, I already answered all these questions. That Pete Lambert, he and Ethan Trask, they were here bright and early after some kids found Lenore's body." He slumped against the door frame. "Nothing I know will help anyone figure out what happened to her. She and I didn't get along so good. She is—she was—an independent sort of woman. Believed she was right about everything." He paused. "Always said I didn't pull my weight in our marriage. Hell. Maybe she was right about that. She was a pretty heavy weight to compete with. But no way did I kill her."

I nodded. "Thank you, Mr. Pendleton." I even added, "I'm sorry for your loss."

He looked at me. "If you find that jewelry, remember. It's mine."

Chapter 23

Children, like tender osiers [willows], take the bow
And as they are fashioned always grow
For what we learn in youth, to that alone
In age we are by second nature prone.

—Verse from John Newbery's
A Little Pretty Pocket-book Intended for
the Amusement of Little Master Tommy
and Pretty Miss Polly (1744), thought
to be among the first books for
children. (The original author of the
verse is Roman poet Juvenal.)
Stitched by Abigail Donnell of York,
Maine, when she was thirteen, in 1815.
Abigail died in childbirth in 1832.

I headed back to Haven Harbor.

I made a quick stop at the patisserie, welcomed Henri back, and bought French bread to

have with the cheeses Gram had brought from Quebec.

She was letting herself in the front door when I drove into the driveway. Perfect timing.

We settled ourselves at the kitchen table in our usual places and she poured us each a glass of pinot noir as I sliced the bread and unwrapped the cheeses she'd brought back: a spicy cheddar, a blue, Camembert, herbed feta, and several varieties I'd never heard of but that smelled wonderful.

Juno happily joined us, going from one of us to the other. Cats didn't show emotions the way dogs did. But Juno was clearly glad Gram was home.

I wondered if she'd be as happy when she got out of her cat carrier at the rectory later today. We all had adjustments to make to Gram's marriage.

"What were the highlights of your trip?" I asked, raising my glass to Gram. Then I smeared decadently creamy blue cheese on a piece of French bread.

"Highlights? Drinking champagne in the bar overlooking the St. Lawrence River at the Château Frontenac. Window shopping at the little shops on the Rue du Petit-Champlain. Visiting the Musée de la Civilisation and playing with all the interactive exhibits. Dinner at le Saint-Amour. I don't even have words for how good that was. Although I don't think we had a bad meal the whole time we were there," Gram said.

"Sounds fantastic," I said.

"When I'm more organized I'll show you

pictures. I can't believe I've lived in Maine all my life and never been to Quebec. Tom and I've already decided we want to go back on our first anniversary." Gram sipped her wine and then sat back. "Now. What's been happening here? Did you learn anything more about Mary Clough's needlepoint? I'm looking forward to seeing it."

I took a deep breath. "I can't show you the needlepoint now. It was stolen."

"Stolen?" Gram looked at me. "From here?"

"No. I gave it to Lenore Pendleton, so she could keep it in her safe." It was hard not to be blunt, but I forged ahead. "The needlepoint, and jewelry that was also in her safe, was stolen when Lenore was murdered."

"Murdered? Lenore? When did that happen?" Gram had put down her glass and looked shaken.

"Late Wednesday night or early Thursday morning."

"I can't believe it. Lenore gone," Gram said. Then she looked closely at me. "You're not getting involved in the murder investigation, are you? You know that's for Ethan and Pete to do."

"I know," I said. Gram hadn't been enthused when I'd gotten involved in other police cases. Truthfully, the police hadn't been thrilled either. "I'm not investigating Lenore's murder. But I have been trying to find out what happened to the needlepoint. It was my responsibility."

Gram looked at me. "It wasn't your fault it was stolen. You put it in the safest place you could think of. And Mary agreed it should be in Lenore's safe, right?"

"She did," I admitted. "But I still feel responsible. I'm guessing whoever took it didn't even know it was old needlepoint. I don't know what it's worth. Mary values it because of its connection to her family."

"Of course," said Gram. "Good for her. Sounds like she has her head solidly on her shoulders."

We sat comfortably quiet for a few minutes, eating our bread and cheeses and sipping wine.

"When I talked to you earlier this week you said there were stories connected with Mary Clough's family and house."

"Have been for years," Gram agreed.

"She told me about her ancestor who was supposed to have tried to rescue Marie Antoinette."

"That story's been around Haven Harbor for over a hundred years. There may be truth in it. Back in those times we Americans were great friends of the French people. After all, Lafayette helped us win our revolution. But we'd gotten rid of King George. I don't suspect many Mainers in those days would have cheered for anyone who tried to save someone of royal blood. Monarchs were thought enemies of the people. So it makes sense nothing was said about what Captain Clough did back in 1793. I remember my grandmother saying she'd heard the Clough family had framed a piece of cloth that was part of one of Marie Antoinette's gowns. But my grandmother had never seen it, and certainly I haven't." Gram sat back. "Did Mary tell you all that?"

"She told me part of it."

"After all," Gram continued. "She's one of the Marys."

Chapter 24

I was sent for into the Council Chamber, where she herself ordinarily sitteth the most part of the time, sowing at some work or other.

—From a report on Queen Mary Stuart sent back to Elizabeth I on October 24, 1561, by Thomas Randolph, the English envoy to Scotland

"One of the Marys?" I asked. Mary herself had used that phrase. She'd also added that she didn't know what it meant.

"Soon after Captain Clough returned home from his famous trip to France, his wife gave birth to a little girl. The Cloughs named her Mary. It's the English version of Marie, of course. Those who knew about Clough's possible connection to Marie Antoinette assumed he'd named his daughter after the queen. Ever since then, every generation in the Clough family has named at least one daughter Mary. The Mary Clough you know is just the most recent one."

What a wonderful story! Although the Clough family's connection to Marie Antoinette, no matter how tenuous, didn't connect the needlepoint to Mary, Queen of Scots.

Who was, of course, another Mary.

Probably a coincidence. Mary was a common enough name.

Gram got up. "It's time Juno and I got back to the rectory. I'll no doubt be back here often to pick up things, but right now I'm trying to figure out how to find places for my clothes without displacing Tom's. I don't think I'll take anything but Juno today."

My phone was humming. A text was coming in. I ignored it for the moment and helped Gram gather Juno's dishes, litter pan, toys, and the food she hadn't eaten. It took us a couple of trips to my car, since Gram hadn't brought hers. Juno watched us suspiciously.

Then Gram lifted her into her carrier. Juno meowed pitifully.

"She thinks she's going to the vet," explained Gram. "I haven't used her carrier for anything else."

As she was putting Juno in the car I checked my phone.

My message was from Sarah. **Ready to share research re: needlepoint.**

I texted her back that I'd be there in half an hour.

First I was taking Gram and Juno to their new home.

I drove Gram up the street, and then drove home to leave my car.

I wrapped up the cheeses we hadn't eaten and put them in the refrigerator.

Gram was home in Haven Harbor. Not home with me.

Now Juno was gone, too.

Gram had lived alone here for the ten years I'd been in Arizona. I wanted to ask her if she'd revisited all the tough times, all the hard days, as she'd walked through these rooms. But I didn't want her to think I was a wimp.

I was beginning to have a glimmer of why Mary Clough planned to get married and sell her house. A house full of memories was wonderful, if the memories were good ones. But not all my memories were joyful. Probably not all of hers were, either. No one has a perfect life.

I shut the front door, hoping I'd leave those thoughts behind, and walked the few blocks to From Here and There.

Sarah didn't have any customers and she'd started water heating for tea.

I pulled over a chair to join her behind her counter and reached for the bowl of gummy lobsters she stashed there. Yum. I still wasn't a fan of antiques, but I was comfortable in Sarah's cozy store. "So—what have you found out?" I asked as she put loose Earl Grey leaves into a ceramic tea infuser in her red and white teapot and poured in hot water from her electric kettle.

"It should be steeped enough in about three minutes, unless you want yours very strong," she said.

I shook my head. I loved watching Sarah make tea. I could understand why in some countries it was a ceremony. At home, if Gram or I wanted a cup of tea, we poured hot water over a tea bag or two. Sarah treated tea with much more respect.

"I'm glad you're here, and we can talk about something pleasant. Everyone who's stopped in here during the past couple of days has told me about Lenore Pendleton's murder. I didn't know her, but what happened is horrible. Beaten to death in her own office! I've never been nervous about living in Haven Harbor, but I've checked the locks on my doors and windows several times a day since I heard." She paused, and then quoted, "'While we were fearing it, it came— / But came with less of fear / Because that fearing it so long / Had almost made it fair.'"

Emily Dickinson seemed to have written a poem for every occasion.

"It's scary," I agreed. "And sad. And so far as I've heard, Ethan and Pete have no clues about who might have done it."

"You still want us to continue trying to figure out what the embroidery was, and how it got to Haven Harbor?" Sarah said.

"Absolutely. And I'm trying to figure out where it is now."

Sarah gave me a quizzical look. "Trying to solve a crime again?"

"Trying to get Mary's needlepoint back to her," I said firmly.

"I'm not sure what I've found will help," said Sarah. "I've been skimming through my books. Several of the ones Skye West gave us were especially helpful."

Skye West, Patrick's mother, had found a bookcase full of books on needlepoint in the estate they were refurbishing. Since she didn't do needlepoint, she'd given the books to Sarah and me for Mainely Needlepoint. Sarah'd kept the ones about early stitchery since Gram already had most of those in her collection.

"Yes?" I waited a moment before Sarah poured us each a cup (not a mug) of tea.

"Ruth and I were right in thinking of Mary Stuart—Mary, Queen of Scots—immediately," Sarah said, sitting back waiting for her tea to cool. "Her mother-in-law in France was Catherine de Médicis, who'd learned needlepoint when she was a girl in a convent school in Florence, Italy. Catherine encouraged Mary to learn needlepoint. I found a couple of references that said she most often used tent stitch and cross-stitch."

I nodded. "Interesting. So that confirms that Mary Stuart knew how to do embroidery."

"No doubt about that. When she left France for Scotland two of her professional embroiderers went with her. She was also commonly seen stitching through political meetings. People said she stitched with her head down so no courtiers could see her reactions to political propositions."

"Sounds smart."

"She was also probably concentrating on what was being said. After all, she'd spoken French since she was five. She wasn't comfortable with Scottish."

"So she would have known how to write in French," I said, thinking of the note Mary'd found with the embroidery.

"She spoke several languages. But, yes. She was most comfortable with French."

"If she brought professional embroiderers with her from France, how could we tell what stitching she did—and which they did?" I asked.

"The professional embroiderers worked on large pieces, like hangings to surround beds for privacy and warmth. Scots castles weren't exactly cozy! Mary even had hangings made to surround her commode so she had privacy."

Sarah had found details about Mary Stuart's life that Ruth hadn't.

"I'm glad we live now. Indoor plumbing is a real plus," I said.

"Spot on. She may have been smart about embroidery, but she wasn't so smart in knowing whom to trust. First she married her English cousin, Henry, Lord Darnley, who was handsome, younger than Mary, and spent his time partying with his friends. He was the father of her one surviving child. He was also one of those involved in plotting to kill Mary's Italian secretary, Rizzio. Mary was furious with him. They didn't spend much time together after that. Darnley died when a gunpowder explosion blew up the house where he was staying."

"It sounds like a soap opera," I said, sipping my tea as Sarah continued.

"No one knows for sure whether Mary was involved in the plot to kill Darnley, but many thought she was. Especially when three months later she married the Earl of Bothwell, who was almost definitely involved."

"So was she finally happy?"

Sarah shook her head. "The soap opera continued. The Scots people felt Bothwell had taken advantage of Mary. They'd only been married a month before other Scottish nobles tried to capture both Mary and Bothwell. Bothwell fled to Denmark. Mary escaped to Lochleven, a castle on an island, where she was held while the Scottish lords ruled."

"So that's when she was imprisoned?"

"For the first time. She was on the island a little less than a year. The books I have disagree about how much she embroidered there. She did ask for silk threads, according to records. I'd guess she did some stitching, but her mind was on more important issues."

"Like getting off the island, I assume," I said.

Sarah nodded. "And getting her crown back. And, on top of all that, she was pregnant."

"So she had another child."

"She miscarried. And then was forced to abdicate in favor of her son. He was only one when he became James the Sixth of Scotland. But she was still held prisoner. She tried to escape, but was caught. Then she tried again, and sought sanctuary in England from her cousin, Elizabeth the First."

"And that was when her long imprisonment started."

"Exactly. She was held in different castles at different times. Records show she asked for packets and skeins of silk thread and cord, to use to embroider. During this period she embroidered with Bess of Hardwick, who was also known as a talented stitcher." Sarah took a deep breath. "If the embroidery Mary Clough found can be traced I think it must be from that eighteen-year period."

Chapter 25

This Queen continueth daily to resort to my wife's chamber where with [Mary] Seton she useth to sit working with the needle in which she much delighteth and in devising works.

—Letter from the Earl of Shrewsbury, Bess of Hardwick's husband, and Mary, Queen of Scots' jailer, to William Cecil, Elizabeth I's secretary of state, in March 1569

"Wow. What kind of embroidery did she do?"

"The sort I told you about before. Embroidery of natural history designs borrowed from books. And 'emblems'—designs based on fables or Bible verses or Latin mottoes. Books with pictures weren't common in the late fifteen hundreds, but women like Queen Mary and her friend Bess might have had them. The designs they stitched have been traced directly to those wood engravings."

"But wouldn't those books have been available to any wealthy ladies of the period?"

Sarah nodded. "Of course. And to women and girls in convent schools."

"So how could work Mary did be separated from work other women did?"

"Mary had a small staff with her—her ladies-in-waiting, for example. One book said a professional embroiderer was even included in her staff during her imprisonment. He might have prepared her cloth by copying the figure she wanted to embroider. Many pieces attributed to her had shapes outlined in black silk. She'd fill in the stitches with tent or cross-stitch, and add bright colors or silver in chain or braid stitch. Colors and designs were more important to her than different stitches."

"Like that crude bird on Mary Clough's embroidery."

"Exactly. And Queen Mary signed her needlework—not with a pen, but with a needle. Sometimes she stitched the royal arms of Scotland, or her initials, MS, for Mary—or Maria, as she was known in France—Stuart. Or a crown. Or M with an R attached, for Mary or Maria Regina."

I frowned. "I don't remember any letters in our embroidery."

"No. But whoever stitched it included a thistle and a rose and a fleur-de-lis. They could easily represent the countries Mary Stuart had lived in, and where she had claims to the throne. Often she embroidered squares or octagons on fine canvas or linen, which could later be joined to make a hanging. Historians think she didn't embroider large pieces because she was always hoping to be released, or to escape. The largest piece she stitched was a crimson satin skirt embroidered with bright flowers in colored silks with gold and silver threads as a gift for her cousin Elizabeth. On each point of the skirt was a thistle."

"So, do you think our Mary's embroidery is the queen's work?" I asked.

"I'm still doubtful. It's in the right style. But although it's old, it's almost too perfect for a piece stitched in the late fifteen hundreds. I'm wondering if it was done one hundred and fifty or two hundred years ago, by someone familiar with Mary Stuart's work."

"But you don't know for sure," I said, hoping the embroidery was authentic.

"To be sure we'd have to have another piece of her embroidery that had been authenticated, so we could compare them. Considering the resources we have now, we can say there's a possibility that needlepoint was done by Mary, Queen of Scots. But not a probability."

Chapter 26

As Mary these lines has wrought
Lord please to hear her tender thought
O to a child thy grace impart
And write thy name upon her heart.

> —Verse stitched by twelve-year-old
> Mary Skillings of
> West Gorham, Maine, 1828

The next morning was Sunday.

I was tempted to skip services, but that wouldn't have gone over well with Gram and Tom. I sipped a large cup of coffee, dug a skirt out of my closet, and slipped into a back pew in time for the first hymn.

Gram probably would have liked me to join her in the first pew, but I'd barely made it in time. I figured I didn't need to call any more attention to myself. Or to the new wife of the minister.

I did a fast walk-through of the reception after the services, leaving Gram and Tom telling everyone about their honeymoon.

I'd already heard most of it. I had other things on my mind.

At home I turned on the television while I made an easy lunch. The house didn't seem as empty when I could hear voices.

Weather would be brisk but sunny. A fire in Saco. No developments in the Haven Harbor murder of lawyer Lenore Pendleton.

I turned it off before they got to the national news.

Local news was depressing enough.

The word "murder" always reminded me of Mama. If she hadn't been trying to protect me . . . but that case was over.

Then I smelled smoke. I hadn't been paying attention, and the bread I'd planned to toast and then melt one of my Canadian cheeses on was, instead, burning.

Nothing serious, but I felt stupid. I opened the kitchen window and back door to get rid of the smoke, threw the crumpled toast out for the birds, and put two more slices of oatmeal bread in the toaster.

The second time I paid closer attention. I slathered soft blue cheese on the toast and had another cup of coffee. Gram would have suggested I add a fruit or vegetable to the meal, so, in her honor, I peeled a banana for dessert.

I shouldn't have had as much coffee. I couldn't stop thinking about Lenore, and the missing jewelry and needlepoint.

Without expertise, the only other way to prove the embroidery wasn't a copy—an old copy, but still, a copy—would be to establish provenance. A connection between the needlepoint and Mary Clough's house in Haven Harbor.

Ruth hadn't called. She must not have found any connections yet.

And I hadn't found the embroidery.

Ethan and Pete would contact the obvious places someone would try to sell the jewelry: jewelry stores and auctioneers and pawnshops. If whoever had stolen it had removed the stones, they might sell the gold and silver and stones to one of the many Mainers who handcrafted fine jewelry. The police would have all that covered.

But without provenance, no one would buy the needlepoint. An auctioneer, if he dealt in high-end merchandise, probably had a staff to try to identify old stitching. That's what we'd been trying to do. But provenance had to come with the item. It couldn't be faked. Or, at least it couldn't be faked and be legal.

No one legitimate would offer cash for anything of questionable ownership.

Establishing provenance was the key.

But how?

On the Fourth of July Mary'd said she had cartons of family papers. I hadn't asked her about those when I'd seen her Friday. Lenore's death had been a much more immediate concern. I should call Mary again. Sarah had volunteered to help Mary go through her papers, but Sarah was tied to her store. Maybe if I helped Mary we might find a clue to the needlepoint's history.

I wasn't finding clues anywhere else.

The weather forecast was right. It was brisk. I could see the pines swaying in the breezes. But the sun was out, and I was restless. I didn't feel like going through boxes of musty papers on a beautiful July day.

I'd call Mary later. In the meantime, I decided to take a walk.

The harbor was as busy as it usually was on a summer morning. A fleet of small sailboats, probably a sailing class sponsored by the yacht club, bobbed up and down between the Three Sisters Islands and the town. Most lobster boats were at their moorings, which, with the buoys marking traps, spotted the harbor with red and blue and yellow.

I leaned over the railing near the town wharf and tried to relax.

"So, you're checking up on me?"

I turned and found myself face to face with Josh Winslow. "Hi, Josh. Why would I be checking up on you?"

"I seem to run into you a lot."

"It's a small town," I answered. "I'm surprised you're not out with your dad on the *Anna Mae*," I said. "It's a beautiful day."

"Nah. I decided I'd stick around here. Dad can do without me for a day. He has a couple of other guys with him." I wondered how Ob felt about Josh's taking the day off.

I left him standing on the pier and walked

along Wharf Street toward the beach and Haven Harbor Light. How long would Josh stick around Haven Harbor? Jude Curran was going to be disappointed if he took off.

It was close to low tide. Pocket Cove Beach was officially a rocky beach, not a sandy one, but most of the rocks were small pebbles smoothed by the sea. A patchwork of blankets and beach towels marked where families had settled. Several people were in the water, and two small boys were filling red plastic buckets with pretty stones and shells and sea glass washed up onto the beach or caught in the dry rockweed above the high tide line. Treasures to take home.

I was restless, too, like Josh. I didn't feel like sitting anywhere. Instead, I climbed the rocky path beyond the beach that led out to the point where Haven Harbor Light stood, surrounded by wild beach roses not yet in bloom, and a small patch of grass.

The light had been automated long before I'd been born. No one had lived there for years. By October no one would bother to make the steep climb to the lighthouse. But today the small area was filled with people taking selfies or photographing their families in front of the lighthouse or watching waves crash over the rocks below. At low tide the surf wasn't dramatic; it was soothing. I stood for a few minutes and counted the waves, as I had when I'd been a child. The seventh was supposed to be the biggest, but almost never was.

A lot of life was like that. Not the way you were told it would be.

Each wave was separate. Different. But all part of the same pattern.

Four cormorants spread their wings out on an exposed ledge. Cormorants were the only seabirds whose feathers weren't oily. After they dived for their dinners they had to dry out.

A strange result of natural selection.

I decided to climb down the far side of the rocks. That was a more difficult climb. The kind kids challenged each other to make, and parents forbid.

I'd done it dozens of times when I was growing up.

The rocks on that side of the lighthouse hadn't been smoothed by the waves. They were long, sharp ridges formed by hundreds of years of incoming tides cutting into layers of granite shiny with traces of mica and quartz and specks of garnet or obsidian.

The farther down I climbed the more I focused on making sure my every step was on solid rock. Some of the largest rocks were the least stable.

The tide was beginning to turn. Waves were now breaking over higher rocks covered with thick slippery rockweed. I threaded my way around tide pools full of starfish and barnacles and periwinkles and the green algae called mermaid's hair. Broken crab and sea urchin shells gulls had dropped were sprinkled on the rocks.

My feet slipped a few times, but I caught myself. Climbing these rocks had always been a part of my life. Something I did to escape from what was happening in town. Or in my life.

No other climber was even close to where I was. The few others on this side of the Light had stayed up higher, on rocks and ledges that were steadier. Safer.

Now the tide was coming in faster and stronger. I decided to climb a little farther and then go back. Not to would be risky.

One last climb. I pulled myself around a sharp ledge to see the spot where one of the largest tide pools had always been. The spot I'd collected sea urchins and starfish and limpet shells and pieces of sea glass no one else had found.

Today it was where Uma Patel lay, her body half submerged in the tide pool, her black hair mixing with green mermaid's hair.

Around her neck was a sapphire necklace.

Chapter 27

How fair is the rose, what a beautiful flower
In summer so fragrant and gay.
But the leaves are beginning to fade in an hour
And they wither and die in a day.
Then I'll not be proud of my youth or my beauty
Since both of them wither and fade
But gain a good name by performing my duty.

—Poem on sampler by Eleanor Waring,
    aged eleven, at the Young Ladies'
    Academy in Georgetown,
    Washington, DC, 1819

It wasn't easy to recover Uma Patel's body, but the Haven Harbor Fire Department, working with the police, the marine patrol, and the coast guard, managed to get her on her way to the medical examiner's office in Augusta before the incoming tide swept her away.

I hid out at the police station to avoid the television cameras and reporters wanting to ask questions of the person who found the body.

"So you were just climbing the rocks, and there she was," said Pete, looking down at the statement he'd asked me to write out.

"Yes," I answered. I wasn't a suspect. But I still felt a little defensive. Was it my fault I'd been the one to find Uma Patel? I hadn't even known she was missing.

When I'd found her body I called Pete directly. I figured he'd know exactly who to go to. If I called 911 they'd notify everyone possible, and the whole town would figure out what was happening before the police had a chance to decide what to do.

I'd made the right decision.

I'd been there through the whole process. And through Ethan's decision that no one would mention the necklace Uma was wearing.

I was pretty sure my first guess was right. It was sapphires. While I was talking to Pete, Ethan was searching Uma's room at the Wild Rose Inn. Mrs. Clifford hadn't hesitated to give him permission to look. This publicity wasn't the sort she was looking for.

But something rang false.

"Are you sure the necklace she was wearing was the same one stolen from Lenore Pendleton?" I asked Pete.

"We're assuming so," he said. "We have pictures of Lenore wearing that necklace."

That necklace put Uma at the top of their suspect list.

A suspect who couldn't be questioned.

But Uma as thief and murderer didn't make sense to me. "How would a tourist from Massachusetts even know Lenore had jewelry in her safe? Much less kill her for it?"

Pete shook his head. "I'll admit pieces of the puzzle are missing. Not to mention other pieces of the stolen jewelry."

"And the needlepoint," I put in.

"And that. That's why Ethan's searching her room at the inn."

"Why would she wear an identifiable necklace stolen from a murder victim? Not to mention that wearing any sapphire necklace to climb rocks seems odd."

Pete shook his head. "I don't know the answers, Angie."

"She looked as though she'd been in the water for a while. And she was in a place that's covered at high tide," I added.

"We'll see what the medical examiner says," Pete said. "But I agree she'd been dead at least one or two tides. Maybe she fell on the rocks and got wedged so the tide covered her, but didn't move her body far."

I looked at him. We'd both grown up in Haven Harbor. We knew the tides and rocks.

"Okay. So that's unlikely in that spot," he admitted. "But until we have the official word on how she died and when, it's all we have to go on. You knew she was staying at the Wild Rose Inn," he continued, taking notes.

I did. So did they. It was in their records, from

their interview with Uma the morning she and Rob had found Lenore's body.

"Mrs. Clifford at the inn said you'd visited Ms. Patel there Friday morning."

"Yes. I did," I said.

"How did you know her?"

"I didn't," I admitted. "But I'd heard she'd been with Rob when he discovered Lenore Pendleton's body. I wanted to hear her story about why she was there, and what they'd seen."

"Angie, you weren't supposed to be questioning witnesses," said Pete, looking more frustrated than angry.

"I didn't ask her about the body, although she did seem shaken at having found it. I asked her about the needlepoint."

"But she didn't see the needlepoint." Pete paused. "Lenore was already dead. The needlepoint was gone."

"Right. But she'd gone there because she wanted to see it. She'd met Josh and Arvin and Rob and Jude Curran at the Harbor Haunts Tuesday night. Rob was bragging about the embroidery. Said it was old and valuable. Uma told me she hoped that if she could identify a special piece of needlepoint, it might prove her worth to the museum where she worked."

"So she knew about the needlepoint the night before." Pete was taking notes.

"She knew about it Tuesday night. By Wednesday night she must have known where it was—Rob must have told her—because by then she'd made arrangements to meet him Thursday morning to go to Lenore's office and see it."

"And this needlepoint is valuable?"

"At first we thought it might have been done by Mary, Queen of Scots. Now we're not as sure."

Pete looked blank. He'd attended Haven Harbor schools, too. We hadn't spent a lot of time studying Elizabethan England. "And if that's so, it would be worth a lot?"

"Maybe," I said. "Uma might have known more."

"When you talked to her, did she say anything about the missing jewelry?"

"No. I did notice she was wearing a pair of sea glass earrings, though." I was pretty sure sea glass earrings weren't the kind Lenore had kept in her safe. "She was excited about going lobstering with Arvin that afternoon."

"Lobstering?"

"She'd told the guys she didn't know much about it. Arvin had invited her to go out with him on his boat Friday afternoon while he hauled a few traps. Show her how it was done."

"The ME said Lenore was killed at about midnight the night before Rob and Miss Patel found her," mused Pete. "I wonder where Ms. Patel was then."

"Earlier that evening Sarah Byrne and I saw her at the co-op with the same group she'd been with Tuesday night at the Harbor Haunts."

"When was that?"

"About eight o'clock," I said. Four hours before Lenore's murder.

"I don't know where she was then," said Ethan, joining the conversation as he walked into Pete's office. "But right now she's pretty high on our suspect list. We found a bag of jewelry in her hotel room, in one of her suitcases. I'll have to compare it to the list Glenda Pierce made, but it sure looks to me like pieces that belonged to Lenore Pendleton."

"Was any needlepoint in her room?" I asked.

"No. Just a few bags of souvenirs from local shops, a box from the patisserie, and a couple of Kate Flora mysteries. The jewelry was in a pocket of her suitcase. Not even well hidden," said Ethan. "But if she didn't kill Lenore Pendleton, how did the jewelry get there? And why was she wearing that sapphire necklace?"

Chapter 28

The rose is red
The leaves are green
The days are past
That I have seen.

—Sampler stitched by Julia Ann Forbs,
   Wooster, Ohio, 1827

I didn't know what else to say, and Pete didn't have any more questions. He volunteered to drive me to the rectory. I didn't want to be alone, and I didn't want to talk to the newspeople who knew where I lived and were staking out my house.

Rev. Tom had volunteered to work with the police. They were trying to locate Uma Patel's parents. Gram'd already heard I'd been the one to find Uma's body.

She must have been watching for me; she opened the door before I had a chance to knock. "Heavens, Angel, what a horrible day you must be having. Come in, sit down, and tell me what happened."

I followed Gram into her kitchen. Food was everywhere.

"You've been shopping," I said, looking around. "A lot of shopping."

"Actually, no," she said. She looked a little embarrassed. "It seems a clergyman belongs to his parish maybe even more than he does to his wife. All this food was here when we got home Friday night. He'd called his secretary to tell her he was coming home, and she must have alerted the Ladies' Guild. They left a note saying they didn't want us to worry about cooking for a few days." Gram shook her head. "The freezer is full of enough casseroles to last us a month. You'd be doing us a favor if you took a few. We'll have to sneak them out, though, so no one thinks we're discarding food made for us."

I looked around the room. A large box from the patisserie. Boxes of store-bought crackers. A platter of brownies. A plate of oatmeal cookies. Bottles of root beer, Tom's favorite nonalcoholic drink. A box of chocolates. Nuts. A chocolate cake lettered "Welcome Home!" in red frosting. And a basket of fruit wrapped in cellophane.

I picked up a brownie. Fudge and walnuts. Not bad.

"The refrigerator's full, too," Gram said. "We brought cheeses home with us. But there must have been six pounds of locally made cheeses already in there. Plus milk and butter and fresh vegetables."

"What are you going to do with all of it?"

"I told Tom we should take it to the food bank, but he said we couldn't—the ladies would be insulted. They'd think we'd rejected their cooking. So we'll eat as much as we can and return the dishes with thank you notes. We'll take the packaged food to the food bank and make a contribution with the money we would have spent on food ourselves." Gram looked as flustered as I'd ever seen her.

Then we both started laughing. It felt good.

"I'll bet you haven't had anything to eat today, either," she said, once we'd wiped our eyes.

"The brownie was good," I admitted. "Before that? I had toasted cheese and a banana for lunch a while ago."

"Well, you came to the right place," Gram said drily. "Sit down, and I'll find us something to eat besides brownies. Then you can tell me everything that happened today."

Gram might be Mrs. Tom McCully now, but she was still Gram. Eat first, talk later.

It felt good to sit. I hadn't realized how uptight I'd been.

Gram put water on to boil, made us each sandwiches of herbed cheese and fresh sliced tomatoes and lettuce with thin slices of ham, put a bowl of potato chips on the table, and handed me a cup of tea. I took a sip. The tea wasn't made with just milk and sugar. I looked up at her.

"Figured you could do with a bit of brandy,

after what you've been through today," she said. "And I'm joining you. I may be a minister's wife, but I'm still me."

I raised my cup to her, and we ate in companionable silence.

Gradually I explained what had happened. I hesitated about telling her about the sapphire necklace, but then decided that, knowing Haven Harbor, she'd hear the news from someone else. Tom might be hearing it as we talked. And she wouldn't pass the information on.

"Do you think this young woman killed Lenore and stole her jewelry and the needlepoint?" Gram asked.

"The evidence is there. How did the jewelry get into her room at the Wild Rose? But she didn't impress me as a murderer."

"They don't all wear labels, you know," Gram cautioned.

"I do know. But she seemed genuinely upset when she talked about finding Lenore's body. And why would she agree to go with Rob to Lenore's office if she'd already killed her?"

"She'd have to have been pretty tough and smart to arrange to discover her own victim," said Gram.

"Plus, Lenore was wearing nightclothes when she was found. You knew her better than I did. Would she have opened her door late at night to someone she didn't know?"

"I wouldn't think so," said Gram. "Although she'd be more likely to open it to a young woman than she would to a man."

"True," I agreed.

"But if Uma was smart enough to talk herself into Lenore's house close to midnight, and get Lenore to open her safe . . . wouldn't she be too smart to flaunt jewelry she'd stolen by wearing it? A sapphire necklace doesn't look like sea glass." I shook my head. "The last time I saw her she was excited about going out on the *Little Lady* with Arvin Fraser to see how he lobstered. That was Friday, late morning. She was going to meet him Friday afternoon."

"Did you tell the police that?' Gram asked.

"I did. I'm sure they'll talk to Arvin."

Gram sat back. "I don't want to think ill of anyone, but I'm disappointed in Arvin Fraser. I don't know the man well. I do know his wife's mother, though, and I've heard he's having marriage issues. Married too young and a father too soon. He's not the only one ever to be in that position. But to invite a young woman he hardly knew out on his boat doesn't sound smart to me."

I shrugged. "I don't know his wife. But I have heard they're having problems. Sarah and I saw Uma with Arvin, Josh, and Rob down at the Harbor Haunts after the fireworks. Jude Curran was there, too. And the same group was together the next night at the co-op."

"That was the night Lenore was killed, right? The night they were at the co-op?"

"Right."

"What time was that?"

I thought back. "I told Pete about eight or so. Rob, Josh, and Jude were still there when we left.

I don't know where Arvin or Uma were. I don't remember seeing them out on the pier."

"And about four hours after that Lenore opened her door to her killer."

"That's right."

"So the question is, where did all those people go after you saw them at the co-op?" said Gram.

A good question. The same one Pete had asked.

Along with finding out how Lenore's jewelry had gotten into Uma's room. And around her neck.

Chapter 29

While rosy cheeks your bloom confess
And youth your bosom warms
Let virtue and let knowledge dress
Your mind in lighter charms.

—Sampler stitched by twelve-year-old
   Elizabeth Kindrick of Saco, Maine, 1812

I spent the rest of the afternoon and evening with Gram. We chatted about her trip, she showed me dozens of pictures she'd taken in Quebec, we watched Juno race around the house and make herself at home, and most of all, we tried to think about things other than death. Tom stayed at the police station.

They'd called Uma's family, he told us when he checked in with Gram. Her parents were on their way to Maine from their home in Connecticut. Tom had arranged for them to stay at the

Wild Rose, and made other telephone calls for them. He and Pete had also promised to try to keep the press away.

That wouldn't be easy. Word had already gotten out about the sapphire necklace Uma'd been wearing. The only thing worse for parents to hear than that their daughter was dead would be that their daughter might have been a murderer and thief. I couldn't imagine how they must feel.

Welcome to quiet, peaceful Haven Harbor.

I went back to my own house for the night (taking backyard routes to avoid the media), but sleep didn't come easily.

I kept seeing Uma Patel's body on the rocks, sapphires sparkling through the seaweed that partially covered her.

I still couldn't believe she'd killed Lenore, even with that evidence.

Could she have been with whoever had killed Lenore?

She'd said she didn't know anyone in Haven Harbor except Arvin, Josh, and Rob. And Jude.

But if she'd met someone else, would she have told me? I'd only asked her about finding Lenore's body. I hadn't asked her the names of everyone she'd met in Haven Harbor.

How had Uma ended up dead, her body cast ashore on the rocks?

I thumped my pillow and turned over. My thoughts shifted between Uma, and her death, to Lenore, and hers. Two people who didn't seem to have anything in common—except a sapphire necklace.

And why hadn't the needlepoint been with the jewelry Ethan found in Uma's room?

What did that mean? Uma wouldn't have tossed it out as not important. She'd have put it in a safe place.

Finally I sat up and started a list. Making lists was an old habit. If my mind was too churned up to let me sleep, I wrote down what was bothering me. That got the problem out of my mind and let me relax.

As a teenager I'd made lists of the boys I'd liked and the ones I hadn't. The girls who were mean, and the ones I trusted. The places I wanted to visit someday. My favorite colors. What clothes I'd buy if I had a million dollars.

Lists helped me focus.

I wrote the word "Motives" at the top of the page.

The person with the strongest motive to kill Lenore seemed to be her almost-ex-husband, Charlie. He might inherit, if she hadn't changed her will. As her husband, he might get something, even if she'd rewritten her will. He had a history of drinking and violence. Would Lenore have let Charlie in?

She might have. He had been—was still, legally—her husband, after all. And Glenda had said that, despite Charlie's annoying her, Lenore hadn't been afraid of him.

But, on Charlie's side, if he'd killed his former

wife he would have taken her jewelry. He knew how much it was worth. He wouldn't have given the jewelry to someone else, like Uma. He wouldn't have cared about the needlepoint.

That jewelry again. How had Lenore's jewelry gotten into Uma's room?

I couldn't imagine anyone who would give her the jewelry except Lenore, under duress.

What if I forgot that the jewelry was ornamental? What if I only considered its value?

Plenty of people I'd spoken to wanted money. Rob, of course, wanted to buy a lobster boat. According to Cos and Mary, Jude wanted to start over, in another place. So did Josh. Arvin was having marital problems and was still paying off his boat. He might have been tempted by easy money. It would give him other options.

But, then, who wasn't interested in money? Even Henri and Nicole were worried about not having enough money to move his mother to Maine.

Usually making a list kept my mind from racing. Tonight's list kept me awake. I turned off my bedside lamp and tried, again, to sleep.

I'd finally fallen into a deep sleep when my telephone rang at seven-thirty. Groggily I reached out to where I'd left my phone, on my night-stand. It was Ruth.

"Angie? I hope I didn't wake you. I heard about your finding that poor girl's body yesterday."

"Yes," I said, struggling to wake up.

"What an awful thing that must have been. How are you doing?"

"I'm all right," I said. "I spent yesterday afternoon and evening with Gram."

"I'm so glad you weren't alone," Ruth continued. "If I'd known earlier it was you who found that girl, I would have invited you over here."

"Thank you for thinking of me. But I'm all right," I said. I hoped that was true.

"I know you have other things on your mind. But when you get a chance, maybe you could stop in. I've been working on that research you asked me to do—to connect Mary, Queen of Scots, with Marie Antoinette? And I think I've got it."

By then I was wide awake. "What is it?"

"It's a little complicated. But I've written it all out. It would be easier to explain in person."

"In about an hour?" An hour would give me enough time to shower and drink coffee.

"An hour will be fine. I'll see you then."

I dragged myself out of bed. Lenore's jewelry had been found, but not Mary's needlepoint. Maybe I shouldn't even still be trying to trace its provenance. But I'd promised Mary I would. I wanted to honor that promise.

I'd also promised to get her needlework back to her. I hadn't gotten very far with that. But I hadn't given up.

One hot shower, two cups of coffee, and three pieces of French bread slathered with brie later, I was on my way to Ruth's little white house in the shade of the Congregational Church's steeple. I passed the rectory on my way. I hoped Tom had finally gotten home last night. If he hadn't, at least Gram had Juno to keep her company.

But she wouldn't mind being alone. She would've supported Tom's decision to be where he was most needed. She was going to be a great minister's wife.

Chapter 30

Last night there were four Marys,
Tonight there'll be but three;
There was Mary Seton and Mary Beaton,
And Mary Carmichael and Me.

—First verse of an eighteenth-century
English ballad that combines two
historical events. The four Marys who
served Mary, Queen of Scots, were Mary
Seton, Mary Beaton, Mary Fleming, and
Mary Livingston; no Mary Carmichael.
Mary Hamilton, the subject of the ballad,
was a Scots woman who served Catherine,
the wife of Peter the Great, of Russia.
Mary Hamilton was executed for killing her
illegitimate child, whose father was the tsar.

Ruth was waiting for me in her dining room/
study. Pieces of paper, some she'd written on,
and some she'd printed out from the computer,

covered her dining room table. I looked, aghast.

"Ruth, I hadn't realized I'd asked you to do this much research!"

She patted a chair seat for me to sit on. "Don't worry. It was fun. I used to do research for all my books because they were set in different periods in history—usually English history. That was in the old days, when I wrote romances that had 'erotic components.' Now my books have more sex and less history. Got to please the market, you know. I enjoyed the excuse to stop focusing on sex and go back to thinking about history."

I sat down next to her. "So—what did you find?"

"Mary of Scotland and Marie Antoinette both went to France from other countries because of international alliances. They were both queens of France. Marie Antoinette, of course, was queen of France when she was executed. Mary of Scotland returned to Scotland and then ended up in England, where she also had a claim to the throne. She was executed there."

"Yes?" I said. So far I'd known all that, although I hadn't pulled the details together the way Ruth had. I hoped she hadn't gotten so fascinated with historical minutia that she'd forgotten what she was looking for. "And . . . so?"

"The note with the needlepoint was written in French, so I decided to focus on French connections."

I half smiled. I might not know much about history, but I'd seen the movie *The French Connection*. I didn't remember any needlepoint involved in that story.

"I won't bore you with the details," Ruth went on, "but one of the reasons Mary of Scotland ended up in France was that her mother, Mary of Guise, was French. She'd left France to marry James the Fifth of Scotland. James died only a week after their daughter Mary was born. Mary of Guise was the one who arranged for her young daughter, Mary, who was now the queen of Scotland, to go to France and marry the heir to the French throne. Mary of Guise was a staunch Catholic. One of her sisters, in fact, was the abbess at the Convent of Saint-Pierre-les-Dames in Reims."

"Another Mary," I said, thinking of what Mary Clough had told me. "Mary, Queen of Scots, and her mother were both Marys."

"And they weren't the only ones," Ruth said, nodding. "Of course, while she was in France Mary Stuart was called Marie, as was Marie Antoinette, two centuries later. She and her ladies received part of their education at the abbey in Reims, where her aunt was the abbess. They also visited the abbey after Mary's husband, Francis the Second, died."

"That would make sense. The abbess was her aunt, and Mary and her mother's family were all Catholics," I said. I was beginning to understand the history a little. But I still didn't know how it connected to the needlepoint. And it was hard to keep all the Marys straight. Hadn't Elizabethans used any other names? I must have started to look restless, because Ruth reached out and touched my arm.

"Don't be impatient. I'm almost to the key

part." She pointed at a printout of an English folk song. "There were other Marys. Four others, to be exact. When five-year-old Mary Stuart was sent to France to prepare to be the French queen, her mother wanted her to retain ties to Scotland. She chose four other girls, all named Mary, from families in Scotland that she knew and trusted, to be Mary Stuart's ladies-in-waiting."

I shook my head. "So Mary Stuart and four other Marys went to France. Weird. You'd enter a room and ask for Mary—and five girls would answer!"

"Precisely. Which is why they all had informal names, too. Mary of Scotland was, of course, *the* Mary or Marie. Mary Fleming was nicknamed La Flamina. Mary Beaton was called Beaton, and Mary Seton was called Seton. Mary Livingston was known as Lusty, because she was strong and athletic. All four grew up with Mary Stuart. After Mary's husband died they all went back to Scotland with her. Mary Livingston, Mary Beaton, and Mary Fleming all married men loyal to Mary Stuart."

"What about the fourth Mary?"

"Mary Seton was the closest of the four to Mary Stuart. After they returned to Scotland she was put in charge of the queen's household, and she stayed with the queen, and even went into captivity with her."

"Never married?"

"She was asked, so history says, but she chose to remain single. And she may be the connection with Mary Clough's needlepoint." Ruth looked very pleased with herself. But I still didn't get it.

"Mary Seton? How?"

"As I said, she went into captivity with Mary Stuart. She arranged Mary's hair and wigs, did needlepoint with her, and looked after her wardrobe. But after fifteen years she became ill. Her family, and Mary Stuart herself, advised her to leave England and its drafty castles and go somewhere more comfortable, and better for her lungs."

"And so she left?"

"She did." Ruth nodded. "In 1583 she returned to France, and went to live at Saint-Pierre-les-Dames at Reims—the same abbey she'd visited as a child, where Mary Stuart's aunt was the abbess. Mary Seton lived there for the rest of her life."

I was waiting for the needlepoint connection. "And?"

"Mary Stuart was known to be generous with her friends and staff. Even in the hectic days before she was executed she made provisions for her servants, her friends, and her relatives. She had little money, but she left instructions as to which of her needlepoint pieces should be given to each person. Mary Seton was a close friend. I'm wondering if that note in French was from Mary Stuart . . . who would have called herself Marie in French . . . to Mary Seton. And if it accompanied a piece of needlepoint she stitched as a remembrance for Mary Seton to take with her to France."

"When Nicole translated the note she did say

it looked as though it was addressed to someone whose name began with an *S*," I said, remembering. "So, okay, the needlepoint could have been done by Mary, Queen of Scots, and taken to France by Mary Seton. But that still doesn't connect with Marie Antoinette!"

"No. But if the abbey of Saint-Pierre-les-Dames had a piece of needlework stitched by a queen, I would think they would value it highly and preserve it," said Ruth. "And there was a connection between Marie Antoinette and the abbey. Marie Antoinette's lawyer, who defended her at the trial where she was condemned to death, was Guillaume Alexandre Tronson. He was from Reims."

"And obviously closely connected to the court of Marie Antoinette," I said.

"Exactly. At that time the archbishop of Reims was Alexandre-Angélique de Talleyrand-Périgord. We remember him just as Talleyrand. He left France during their revolution and spent time in the United States. In 1794 he even visited Maine. Later, of course, he went back to France. But he knew Tronson du Coudray. By the time of the French Revolution the abbey where Mary Seton had lived was gone, and its treasures had been incorporated into those of the cathedral at Reims. Given the destruction that took place during the French Revolution, wouldn't it have been reasonable for the archbishop at the cathedral, Talleyrand, to entrust the church's treasures to someone leaving the country? Perhaps he was protecting the church's assets. Or perhaps he gave them away as bribes."

"And you're suggesting that Mary Clough's needlepoint might be one of those treasures removed from the cathedral by Talleyrand."

"And perhaps given to du Coudray, and passed on to Captain Clough," Ruth continued.

"Wow," I said. "I'm going to need you to write that all down—the names and the dates especially."

"I've already done that," said Ruth, handing me a sheet of paper. "Now all we have to do is connect the Clough family of Haven Harbor to Talleyrand or du Coudray. James Swan, the Boston investor who connected Captain Clough to royalists in France, knew Talleyrand. And in 1794 Talleyrand visited Henry Knox, in Rockland, and also went to Gardiner and Augusta, here in Maine, so he's the likeliest to have visited Haven Harbor. Du Coudray died in Africa. He never made it to the states."

"The papers in Mary's house might have clues," I said. "I need to talk to her."

"And, of course," Ruth added, "we still don't know where that needlepoint is. I heard Lenore's jewelry was found in the room where that poor girl who drowned was staying."

Word had gotten around town quickly.

"Yes," I confirmed.

"But not the needlepoint?"

"No. Not as far as I've heard," I answered. "And if Uma had it, I don't think she would have discarded it. She'd have left Haven Harbor immediately and gone back to Boston. She wouldn't have stayed around to go lobstering with Arvin Fraser." Or die in Haven Harbor, I added to myself.

"I hope the police are talking to Arvin," Ruth said. "He may have been the last person to see her alive. He might know her plans. Or what she'd already done."

I nodded. "I'm sure they'll talk to him. The question is, what will they find out?"

Chapter 31

When I am dead
And laid in Grave
And all my flesh decayd
When this you see
Pray think on me
A poor young harmless maid.

—Stitched by Rachel Anderson,
ten years old, 1803

"Angie? This is Ethan. Ethan Trask."

He didn't have to tell me who he was. I'd recognized his voice since I was twelve and he was sixteen. Not that I wanted him to know that.

"Yes?"

"Any chance you'd have time to talk? I have loose ends that need to be tied up. I thought maybe you could help."

Time to talk to Ethan? Just the rest of my life.

"Sure, Ethan. Shall I come down to the police station?"

Pete was the cop who listened to me. For Ethan to call was suspiciously different.

"Truth is, this place is a little crazy now. Media, you know. Unless you want to talk to the world about how you found Uma Patel's body."

I shuddered. "No, thanks."

"Then what about meeting at Harbor Haunts for a burger? It's close to lunch time, and I need to get out of this office."

"I can be there in fifteen minutes," I answered.

"See you there."

I'd just gotten home from talking with Ruth. My head was full of English and French history. But it didn't take me long to check the mirror in the front hall. A comb and a lipstick would make a major difference in how the world saw me.

I even changed my T-shirt. I might not be royalty, like those Marys, but I knew how to please my Haven Harbor public.

Dressing up more than putting on lipstick and a new T-shirt for lunch at the Harbor Haunts would have felt odd.

I was standing outside the door of the café in sixteen minutes. I wasn't even out of breath. Much.

Ethan rounded the corner from the street where, several blocks away, the Haven Harbor Police Station had stood for as long as I remembered. We were a small town, with a small police presence. But Pete Lambert and the others who worked there always made space for Ethan when he was working a murder investigation in the Harbor. Which recently had been all too often.

He looked good. Over six feet tall. A light tan, which in Maine meant he spent some, but not all, of his time outside. The same amount of time outside without sunblock in Arizona would have resulted in sunburn or permanent charring. And those blue eyes . . . Not that the rest of him wasn't pretty darn good. But those eyes were what always got to me.

Lucky wife. I'd never met her, but if Ethan had chosen her, she must be pretty special. I wondered when her unit was coming home. But I didn't ask.

"I'm starving. Hope you don't mind discussing bodies while we eat," he said, opening the Harbor Haunts door for me.

"No problem," I answered. Not if he was on the opposite side of the table.

We were early enough to find a corner table with a view of Main Street. Like all cops, Ethan sat with his back to the wall, facing the door. I suspected he even did that when he went out for dinner with his wife and daughter.

We each ordered cheeseburgers; mine rare, his well done.

So—he liked charred meat. He wasn't perfect.

Sweet potato fries for me; regular fries for him. "And iced coffee," he added. I decided not to have the beer I'd been thinking about. "Iced tea," I said. I'd have a beer later.

"Sorry to bother you," Ethan said. "But you've been talking to people around town about that missing embroidery."

"I still feel responsible for its disappearing."

"While you've been doing that, you've also been talking to people who may be involved with Lenore Pendleton's murder."

The waitress put down our food and we both dug in. I hadn't realized how hungry I was.

"You haven't found out anything about the needlepoint, have you?" he asked.

"Several people were interested in it, mainly because they thought it might be valuable. Your brother, Rob, wanted to sell it, but I don't think he would have stolen it. He'd either have convinced Mary to sell it, or tried to find other ways to make the money he was looking for." I hesitated. "I'm not a big fan of your brother, Ethan. He's pushing Mary a bit more than she's comfortable with. But that's none of my business."

"No. It's not," Ethan said. "Rob does see the world a little more in black and white than he should. But he's young. He'll learn. I can't believe he'd kill anyone."

"I agree." And I did agree. I still wasn't Rob's biggest fan.

"Who else besides Rob?"

"Uma Patel, you know about. She hoped it would help her get a permanent job at the Museum of Fine Arts. Arvin Fraser and Josh Winslow knew about the needlepoint and its possible value," I said. "Cos and Jude Curran did, too."

"Because Mary lives with them," Ethan confirmed. "But they had no special interest in needlepoint."

"No. A couple of art dealers from Quebec were here this week." I hesitated. "They were interested in old needlepoint; they asked Sarah if she had any. I saw them talking to Rob and Josh and Jude. But I don't know if they knew about this particular embroidery."

"What are their names?" Ethan took out a small notebook.

I hesitated again. I'd never even met the couple. "Victor Nolin was the man," I said. "Sarah Byrne would know both their names. She also has their address in Canada. They were staying at the Wild Rose Inn. I don't know if they're still there."

The same place Uma had been staying. But Haven Harbor was small. The only other place in town to stay was Mrs. Chase's bed and breakfast, and Skye West had reserved that for herself and her family for the summer, even though she was seldom there.

"Did anyone else know about it?"

I thought a moment. "My grandmother, and the Mainely Needlepointers, whom you know. And Nicole Thibodeau at the patisserie. She translated the letter with the embroidery for us." I ran through everyone in my head. "Charlie Pendleton, Lenore's soon-to-be-ex, was interested in her jewelry. I don't think he knew about the needlepoint."

"Okay. Anyone else?"

"Not that I can think of." I took another bite of my cheeseburger. "Why all the questions? I thought you'd found Lenore Pendleton's killer. Yesterday you sounded pretty sure Uma Patel was responsible."

It still didn't make sense to me that Uma'd done it, but I'd heard the evidence.

"Actually, I didn't want to talk to you about Lenore Pendleton's death." Ethan lowered his voice and leaned toward me. "I wanted to talk to you about Uma Patel."

"I don't know much about her. I only talked with her once before . . . I found her. She seemed bright and ambitious." She hadn't seemed like a killer. But then, killers didn't wear ID bracelets.

"We've confirmed that the necklace Uma Patel was wearing was the one that belonged to Lenore Pendleton. Glenda Pierce even found us a picture of Lenore wearing it," said Ethan.

"And yesterday you said the rest of the missing jewelry was found in her room at the inn."

Ethan paused. "True. But—and this isn't public information, Angie, so don't share it with anyone—her fingerprints weren't on the bag the jewelry was in."

"Whose were?"

"No one's. The bag was clean. And two pieces of Lenore Pendleton's jewelry were not in there."

"Uma was wearing the sapphire necklace."

He nodded. "So we know where that was. But an emerald ring is still missing."

I thought about that for a moment. "So the bag of jewelry may have been planted in her room."

"We're considering that possibility. And we have another, even more serious situation."

I leaned toward Ethan so I could hear him as he lowered his voice.

"The medical examiner says Uma Patel didn't drown."

"What?" I said, moving back. "But I saw her!" I'd seen her body. A body that had been in the North Atlantic and cast up by tides and surf onto a rocky shore wasn't pretty. I hoped her parents hadn't had to see her.

"You saw her on the rocks, where the surf had probably taken her. There's no doubt she was in the water for a day, maybe two. But the ME says she was dead before she went in the water," Ethan continued, picking up a couple of French fries and dipping them in ketchup.

"Have you talked to Arvin?" I asked. "When I saw her Friday she was looking forward to going lobstering with him." I'd found her body on Sunday. Two days later.

"Pete and I both talked to him. He says she was fine Friday. He took her for a short turn around the harbor, hauled a couple of traps, and then left her at the town wharf." He paused. "We're looking to confirm that with anyone who was near the wharf that afternoon, of course."

"Did Uma sleep at the inn Friday night?"

"Mrs. Clifford doesn't know. She saw Uma go out Friday afternoon, and Uma didn't come down for breakfast the next morning. But not every guest does. She assumed Uma had been out late, or was planning to have breakfast with someone else."

"What killed her?"

"The ME found evidence she'd been hit on the head. Several times. If she were walking on the ledges and fell, she might have hit her head. All her injuries were slightly different sizes. Injuries consistent with being hit with an irregularly shaped rock."

"The ME's sure her body wasn't bruised or damaged by the tide dashing it against the rocks?" Rocks along the Maine coast were often sharp and jagged.

"Believe me. I asked the same question," said Ethan. "But he's confident at least some of the blows—the deeper ones that killed her—couldn't have been caused by her slipping on the rocks. She was dead when she hit the water."

"Arvin says she was fine when she left his boat."

"That's what he insists. He says he has no idea how she got in the water." Ethan paused. "And he doesn't think she was wearing a necklace when she left the boat." Ethan shook his head slightly. "Of course, he also doesn't remember what she was wearing or what they talked about or whether she mentioned what she was going to do after she left his boat. But he does insist he didn't kill her."

So he'd been asked.

"Another thing that's funny," Ethan contin- ued. "Most women carry a purse, or backpack, a place to hold their cell phones and credit cards and . . . whatever else women carry. We haven't found any of Uma's belongings."

"If she fell on the rocks—or was hit on the head near there—she would have dropped whatever she was carrying."

"Right. But if she was on dry land to begin with, you'd think we'd have found those things. Of course, if she was on a boat or even a wharf, they might be under the water. In any case, we haven't found them. They weren't near her body, or on the rocks, or on Arvin's boat—yes, we searched it—or in her room at the inn. Nowhere. No license, no money, no credit cards, no keys—to her car or to her room at the inn."

"If someone planted Lenore's jewelry in Uma's room to make her look guilty, they would have needed a key," I said, thinking it through. "Did Mrs. Clifford or any guests at the inn see anyone entering Uma's room?"

Ethan shook his head. "Unfortunately, no. Mrs. Clifford leaves the front door of the inn open from six in the morning until ten at night so her guests don't have to use their keys except to get into their rooms. She has no way of knowing whether guests are in the inn or not—no digital images of keys, no closed-circuit cameras."

I wasn't surprised. The Wild Rose wasn't a Hilton. Mrs. Clifford hadn't expected to need any high-tech security devices. Not until now.

"When I saw Uma Friday morning at breakfast it was about nine-thirty," I said, thinking back.

"She had a small bag with her, on the floor next to her chair. A blue canvas bag. She opened it and gave me her card."

"That's one of the questions I was going to ask you: whether you'd seen her with a pocketbook," he said. "You're right on target. Her parents said she had a blue bag she used when she was away from work. She had a leather bag for work. That one is still in her apartment in Boston. Empty. The police there checked."

"Whoever killed her could have taken the keys and thrown the bag away. Into the water, or into a Dumpster. Anywhere," I said. "Then they could have gotten into her room at the Wild Rose to plant the jewelry." I hesitated a moment. "Or, if Uma killed Lenore and was carrying the jewelry with her, he or she could have taken the jewelry."

"And put it in her room?" Ethan shook his head. "That doesn't make sense."

"And you're sure the embroidery wasn't in her room?" I asked.

Ethan shook his head. "Positive. We're stuck. Arvin's the obvious suspect, but we don't have any proof. Or motive. That's why I wanted to talk to you. I thought maybe you'd heard something that would help pull all this together."

"All I've heard about Arvin is that he and his wife are having problems. They married young and have a baby. Alice thinks he leaves her alone too often. And Arvin owes money on his boat."

Ethan shrugged. "Most young lobstermen pay off their boats slowly. And most wives feel neglected. Those aren't grounds for Arvin to kill anyone."

"A father has responsibilities as well as a mother."

"Sure. But a father who's working has obligations to his job, too. If he's supporting his family and not running around, then he's doing what he can."

"You don't think he needs to be there to support his wife emotionally? Be there when she needs him?"

I didn't think we were talking about Arvin anymore.

"When there's a child involved, both parties have responsibilities to the child. Of course, and to each other. But their child should be the center of their focus."

We stared at each other. I was the one who looked away. Ethan and I disagreed about that. But he was married and had a child. Experience was on his side. Arguing wouldn't get us anywhere.

"Even if Arvin and Alice have problems, that's not a reason for him to kill anyone," I said. "But the missing needlepoint may be valuable. We're getting close to having a complete timeline for possible provenance."

"So the needlepoint was worth stealing," said Ethan.

"The question is—where is it now?"

"All the personal belongings in Uma's room at the inn were hers. Except Lenore's jewelry."

"I don't know if Arvin killed Uma," I said. "Circumstantial evidence certainly puts him in the right place at the right time. Someone must have planted Lenore's jewelry in Uma's room to make people believe she'd killed Lenore. So far as I know, the only time Uma saw Lenore was after she was dead. And I talked to her about that. So did you. I believed her."

"I did, too. I don't know how she got mixed up in something beyond looking at a piece of embroidery," said Ethan.

"If we find that embroidery, we find the murderer," I said. "I can't help thinking Arvin knows details he's not telling you."

"I agree," said Ethan. "It all gets down to that piece of needlepoint."

"Do you have any idea who might have it?" I asked.

He sighed. "Oh, hell. We haven't a clue."

We'd almost finished our lunches. I wasn't sure we'd accomplished anything. I'd learned Uma had been killed before she was in the water. But killed by whom?

"What about Charlie?" I asked as Ethan called for our check. "I'm not convinced the same person murdered both Lenore and Uma. Charlie had a motive to kill Lenore. He'd inherit, and he wanted that jewelry back."

"Her almost-ex?" Ethan shook his head. "He has an alibi. He was in a bar in Bath the evening Lenore was killed. We know, because the Damariscotta Police picked him up on Route One about midnight. He was on his way home, but they decided it would be safer for him and others on the road for him to spend the night at the Lincoln County Jail."

"A pretty good alibi," I had to admit.

"Between you and me, I would've loved it to have been Charlie. He's a danger to himself and others when he's on the road."

"Won't he lose his license for DUI?"

"Are you kidding? He doesn't have a valid license. Doesn't seem to stop him from drinking or driving."

Ethan finished his iced coffee and sat back in his chair. "We don't have anyone else we can connect to Lenore. Maybe her killer was some-one random."

I looked at him. Hard. "Would Lenore open her door late at night to someone she didn't know? She was a smart lawyer!"

"Seems unlikely. But unfortunately none of her neighbors saw anything."

"Did anyone see Uma getting off Arvin's boat?" I asked.

"We haven't checked with everyone in the harbor. You know how many people are wander-ing around down near the town wharf on a week like this. But so far, no one's volunteered any-thing."

It all came down to the embroidery.

Chapter 32

Patty Polk did this and she hated every stitch she did in it. She loves to read much more.

—Stitched by Patty Polk, age nine, Kent County, Maryland, circa 1800

I found Mary with Cos and Jude at the Curran's house. I was surprised Jude wasn't at Maine Waves. Maybe it was her lunch hour.

"Have you found my needlepoint?" Mary asked.

"No. But I'm still working on it," I assured her. "And the police are, too. But we've come close to finding out where the embroidery came from."

"So now you're sure it's valuable," said Jude. "Right?"

"It's not that simple," I said. "Mary, Queen of Scots, might have given it to one of her ladies-in-waiting, Mary Seton, who took it to France when she went to live at an abbey there. Both

Talleyrand and Marie Antoinette's lawyer had close ties to the church connected to that abbey where Mary Seton lived. Either of them could have entrusted the needlepoint, as one of the church's treasures, to Captain Clough. Or Talleyrand could have brought it with him when he visited Maine in 1794 and given it to someone in your family."

"Wow," said Mary. "How can you find out what really happened?"

"I'm not sure," I told her. "I think the next step is going through all those family papers you found."

"That will take forever," she said, looking discouraged. "A lot of them are faded, and the handwriting's hard to read."

"When you first showed us your needlework, Sarah Byrne volunteered to help go through your papers with you. With three of us looking, it shouldn't take too long. We know the time periods to look for and the names that would be significant."

"I guess so," said Mary. She didn't look enthused.

"You and I could start looking at your papers late this afternoon, and Sarah could join us after she closes her store."

Mary nodded. "Okay. I could do that. I do think it's awesome you've found out all that other stuff already. And that there were a lot of Marys involved." She paused. "Mary of Scotland, Mary Seton, Marie Antoinette. My grandmother was named, Mary, too. And her mother."

"My grandmother told me she thinks there's

been a Mary in your family ever since Captain Clough came back from France and named his youngest daughter Mary," I said. "We can look for other Marys in your documents while we're sorting through them."

"That sounds like a lot of work," said Jude, who'd been listening to us. "Isn't the needle-point valuable on its own? Why do you need to go through all those old papers to find out how it got into Mary's attic?"

"It wouldn't be as valuable without prove-nance," I told her. "And we'll write it all out, with where we found the information, so Mary can keep it with her needlepoint. Without a proven connection between the stitching and the Clough family, everything I've told you is just an educated guess." I turned to Mary. "How are you doing with sorting the papers at your house?"

"I haven't done much more than when you saw it," she answered. "I've been spending time with Alice Fraser. She's been upset, and I've been helping her with the baby." She smiled. "He's a cute little fellow, even if he does cry a lot."

"So Arvin's still not helping out a lot at home." Did Alice know Arvin had taken Uma out lob-stering?

Mary shook her head. "Alice says he's busy with the *Little Lady* and doing accounts at the co-op. They're hoping to put a down payment on a house soon, so he's working harder than ever. He's been hauling traps twice as often, and working at the co-op at night."

Those must have been nights other than the

times I'd seen the guys drinking at the Harbor Haunts or the co-op. "Rob must be busy, then, too," I said. "Maybe he'll make enough to put money toward that boat he wants."

"Rob hasn't been going with Arvin recently," said Mary. "They argued about something. Rob's been helping me at the house instead of lobstering."

"Then who's been Arvin's sternman?" I asked.

"Josh has," said Mary, looking sidewise at Jude.

"Josh has big plans, too," Jude said. "He wants to go to California. Any time he doesn't have to work for his dad, he's been working for Arvin." She paused. "The needlepoint would be worth a lot even without all those papers, right?"

I shook my head. "Of course, the embroidery is just as beautiful without documentation. But for insurance purposes, and in case Mary ever needs or wants to sell it, she'll need the paperwork."

"Josh and Arvin are getting to be real buddies," agreed Mary. "But that doesn't help Rob and I pull together money for our house and his lobster boat."

"Not everything that happens is about you and Rob," Jude snapped. "Josh and Arvin need money as much as Rob does."

"Have you set a date for your wedding?" I asked Mary, hoping I could change the subject.

"The first Saturday in October. That'll be two weeks after my eighteenth birthday, so I'll be able to use money my mom and dad left me to cover some of the expenses, like a caterer," she said, smiling.

"Early October is beautiful in Maine," I agreed. "The trees are turning, and the tourists have gone home. Except the leaf peepers, of course."

"That's what we thought," said Mary. "We've made an appointment to talk to Reverend McCully. We have a reservation for the church, but we have to go through premarital counseling."

"I think he does that with all the couples he marries," I said. Maybe Tom could bring up the issues Gram and Lenore and I had about this impending wedding. But, no matter, the decision was up to Mary and Rob, and they didn't seem to be hesitating.

She nodded. "That's what his secretary said. I can meet you about three-thirty this afternoon at my house. Is that okay?"

"Sounds good. I'll let Sarah know we need her help, too."

Chapter 33

An Hour will come when you will bless
Beyond the brightest dreams of life
Dark days of our distress.

—Stitched by Grace Munson, age ten, 1803

Sarah agreed to meet us. "But it may be six o'clock before I can get there," she cautioned. "A customer just called and asked if I had any carnival glass. I bought several pieces at an auction in April, but I've never put them out in the store. I don't even remember what colors and patterns they are. I have to find them and log them into my inventory before the customer gets here. And she won't be here until after four-thirty."

"Carnival glass?" I asked.

"Iridescent glass dishes given as prizes at carnivals or movie theaters during the twenties and thirties here in the states. Most pieces were decorative bowls, of all different sizes and shapes. Even punch bowls and glasses. Most of them are orange. Blue and green and red pieces are the most valuable."

"Whenever you get here is fine," I assured her. "Paying customers come first."

"Shall I bring food? I don't know about you, but I'll be starving by six o'clock."

"I have a little time now, and you're working. I'll bring dinner. Nothing fancy."

"Any food is fine," said Sarah. "It's been a depressing day. Everyone who comes in to my shop wants to talk about Uma Patel or Lenore Pendleton."

"Believe me, I'd like this whole mystery solved, the needlepoint recovered, and time to get back to enjoying the summer," I assured her.

"A-men. I'm trying to get a couple of balsam pillows needlepointed between customers. I've finished one of the lighthouse and started on a Christmas tree. Tourists often look for Christmas gifts or decorations when they're on vacation."

"Thanks. Katie will be home next week, and she's stitching up some, too. I should check with Dave to see how he's doing."

"Whoops! Customers entering. See you at six!"

Since Sarah'd reminded me, I called Dave.

"I was about to call you," he said. "I've finished the cushion covers for Skye West. Is she in town? Or shall I give them to you?"

"She's in Boston most of the time, and last I

heard she was on the West Coast for a meeting.
Why don't you drop them off with me? I'll get in
touch with her," I said.

"How's your needlework investigation going?"
asked Dave. "I've been thinking about you.
There certainly was a lot of activity over at
Lenore Pendleton's place a few days back, and I
wondered about the needlepoint you were going
to leave with her."

"Horrible, isn't it? Her being killed."

"I still can't believe it. The police came here,
asking if I'd seen anything, but I don't stand at
my windows watching other people."

I smiled. Some people in Haven Harbor were
known to do just that. A nuisance if they
were your next-door neighbors, but handy to
talk to during a murder investigation.

"Did you know Lenore?"

"As a neighbor. I never used her legal services.
I was a little worried about her, actually. She had
an ex-husband who got out of hand."

"Charlie. I talked to him. You know him?"

"Not personally. But I've seen him over there,
talking to Lenore. Actually, shouting would be
more like it. He could cause a scene. Once I
called nine-one-one because the yelling was
getting so loud. I was afraid he'd hurt her."

"But she was all right."

"I assume so. I saw her after that, and she
seemed fine."

"Charlie visited her the morning of the day—
or night—she was killed," I said. "But Ethan Trask

told me he has an alibi for the time she was killed."

"I thought I saw Charlie's car there that evening, early," Dave said. "But I could have been mistaken. I didn't pay close attention."

"I don't think the police have any real clues as to who killed her."

"I thought it was that girl from Boston. The one who drowned."

"They're still investigating." I decided not to say anything else. After all, I wanted Ethan to trust me, and he'd told me details about the investigation that hadn't been released to the public.

"It's an awful situation all around. And now the needlepoint is missing?"

"Yes. But Sarah and Ruth think it was done by Mary, Queen of Scots, and brought here in the late eighteenth or early nineteenth century. Sarah and I are going over to Mary Clough's house tonight to help her look through her family's papers. See if we can find a connection from that end."

"Could you use extra help? I'm getting bored needlepointing and gardening, and there isn't even a Red Sox game on tonight."

"That would be great! I'd love us to get through all the papers tonight. It might be fun to go through them together." Fun for some people, anyway. "Who knows what we might find? We'll be looking for specific names or dates or places."

"Tell me where to be and when."

I gave him Mary's address. Then I walked

down to the small store on the end of Main Street that sold basic foods, magazines, and newspapers. With Dave coming, I'd be feeding four of us. Jude might even show up. This afternoon she'd seemed very interested in the documentation.

I picked out packages of sliced ham, cheese, bologna, and roast beef, and large bags of pretzels and chips.

My stop after that was at the patisserie.

"Angie, good to see you. How can I help you today?" Nicole was behind the counter.

"I'd like two loaves of sliced bread—one white and one whole wheat," I said. "And a dozen assorted cookies. How's Henri's mother doing?"

Nicole leaned toward me. "It is sad. She is not well, and I need Henri here. We are trying to figure a way she can come and stay with us. Perhaps we can hire a nurse for the times Henri and I are working."

"I'm so sorry, Nicole."

"I would like for her to be in a nursing home. There she could get good care all the time. I am no nurse," Nicole added. "But nursing homes are so expensive!"

I nodded. I'd had no experience with nursing homes, but I had no doubt she was right.

"How is your research going, with the needlepoint?"

"We're making progress. Thank you again for your help with the translation," I said.

"No problem. So the needlepoint is very old, then?"

"It may be," I said. "But we still have work to do to be sure."

"I would love to see it someday."

"I would love to show it to you," I told her. "But I'm afraid it's missing. Whoever killed Lenore Pendleton must have taken it."

"No! Very sad," Nicole said, shaking her head in sympathy. She finished slicing the bread and putting the two loaves into bags, and was picking out the cookies.

"We hope to get it back, though," I added.

"You know where it is, then?" asked Nicole.

"Not yet. But we're working with the police. I'm sure we'll settle it all soon," I said.

"I see," she said, handing me my change. "I wish you luck, then."

I headed for home, my arms full of food for the evening. I'd add a bottle of soda and a six-pack of beer when I got home. I reminded myself to be sure to tell Nicole when we'd found the needlepoint. She'd seemed very interested and, of course, she'd helped with her translation.

It seemed the whole town was getting involved.

Chapter 34

With Gentle hand your daughters train
The Housewifes various art to gain
Or scenes domestic to preside
The needle wheel and shuttle guide
On Things of use to Fix the Heart
And gild with every graceful art
Teach them with neatest simplest dress
A neat and Lovely Mind to express.

—From sampler stitched in 1817

The door of Mary's house was open. I stepped inside. "It's Angie. I'm here. And I brought food for supper."

"Com'on in! I'll be right down."

I was already in, so I headed for her kitchen and put the meats, cheeses, and drinks in her refrigerator. The half-empty six-pack of Shipyard Ale inside told me she and Rob did occasionally use the house, no doubt for privacy. And she had said he'd been helping her sort through things recently.

I hadn't completely forgotten what it meant to be seventeen-almost-eighteen.

Mary came down the stairs carefully, carrying a large carton. I reached up to help her with it.

"Heavy," I said as together we put it down on the living room floor.

"Paper's heavy," she agreed. "There's one carton like this over in that corner, this one, and another carton upstairs."

"I thought Jude might have come to help," I said.

Mary wrinkled her nose. "Jude isn't interested in helping me clean out. All she's interested in is Josh and getting out of Haven Harbor."

I remembered that feeling.

"I've heard Josh talk like that, too. Are they planning to go together?"

Mary considered. "I haven't asked her. She'd like that. I'm not sure what Josh wants, though. He's not exactly dependable. And right now, since Arvin's been giving him the sternman job most days, Rob doesn't want to talk about either of them."

"Jude did seem very interested in the needlepoint this afternoon, though," I said, getting down on the floor next to the carton.

"She did, didn't she?" Mary thought for a moment. "Even Josh and Arvin asked me about it the other day." She shrugged. "Rob bragged about it right after we first took it to you, but he hasn't mentioned it since it was stolen. I think he blames himself for encouraging me to take it to you. If we'd kept it here, we'd still have it."

I winced. "I still hope we can get it back."

"I hope so, too," she said. "So—what are we looking for in all these books and papers?"

"We need to find the connection between this embroidery, and the Clough family in Haven Harbor, and a cathedral in Reims, France, in the late seventeen hundreds or early eighteen hundreds. I assume most of these papers are connected to your family, so we'll see the name Clough a lot. That won't help by itself, unless it also mentions France. Other names to look for are Talleyrand or Tronson du Coudray or Marie Antoinette."

"I'd like to try to find the other Marys," she said, picking up an early *Webster's Speller* that was on the top of the pile. "You said there'd been a Mary in almost every generation for two hundred years. I'd like to know about the rest of them."

"We'll add that to our search," I agreed. "And Sarah and Dave Percy will join us later today."

"Mr. Percy, from school?" Mary asked.

I nodded.

"They both want to help?"

"They do," I assured her. "And I brought sandwich makings so we can eat here and keep working."

"Thank you, Angie," she said. "I appreciate this."

"No problem," I assured her. "Now, let's get to work."

Most of the books in the cartons were old textbooks, although there were a few novels, a book on maritime law, several American Tract Society morality tales, and two old Bibles. We put the Bibles to one side because they contained lists of family members and Mary wanted to look through them more carefully later. One arithmetic book from 1879 had belonged to a Mary Clough. She kept that one out, too.

We made a pile of ships' logs from the second half of the nineteenth century—later than those we were looking for.

We were about to start on the letters, some tied together, when Sarah arrived.

"Wow! You've done a lot already," she said, seeing Mary and I sitting on the floor surrounded by piles of paper.

"But so far we haven't found anything that helps," I told her. "How did your meeting about carnival glass go?" I felt proud I'd remembered what it was her customer was looking for.

"She bought one six-inch orange bowl in the rose pattern. Turned out she already had two larger bowls in the same pattern, so she was thrilled that it completed her set. But it was a small sale for me." Sarah looked around. "I thought you were bringing food!"

"Food's in the kitchen," I assured her. "Dave's going to join us, too."

"Then let's eat. I'm starved," said Sarah.

"Me too," agreed Mary. "I'm ready to wash my hands and take a break."

We were eating our sandwiches and chips when Dave arrived. At first Mary seemed a little intimidated that one of her high school teachers was sitting in her kitchen. But soon she was calling him by his first name with the rest of us.

We'd almost finished eating when Rob stomped in.

"Mary, do you know where Josh and Arvin are?" he asked, ignoring the rest of us.

"I haven't seen them in days," she said. "Jude might know. She's working. Maine Waves is open until nine tonight. I'm pretty sure she talked to Josh earlier today."

"Thanks," Rob said. He slammed the front door in back of him.

"He's upset about something," I said, reaching for another chip or two before we got back to work.

"He's been angry a lot recently," said Mary. "I don't know why. Arvin seems to be hanging out more with Josh. Even if Rob's getting married and is excited about setting up his own lobstering business, that shouldn't make a difference to their friendship. Arvin's already done both those things, and he still seems to be one of the boys, as they say."

A lot of things in Haven Harbor had changed in the past two weeks.

Chapter 35

One did commend me to a Wife Fair and Young
That had French Spanish and Italian tongue
I thankd him kindly and told him I loved
*   none such*
I thought one tongue for a Wife too much
What love ye not the Larned? Yes, as my Life
A Learned Schollar, but not a Larned Wife.

—Stitched by Lydia Kneeland,
Boston, Massachusetts, 1741

"Let's see if we can find what you're looking for," said Sarah. "You've already gone through a lot."

"Books and some of the ships' log," I agreed. "And we separated out the family Bibles."

"Your grandmother was right. There *are* Marys in every generation," said Mary. "I'm beginning to understand what my grandmother said when she told me I was 'one of the Marys.'"

"We're putting aside anything related to a Mary," I instructed the others. "Even if the reference won't help us identify how the needlepoint got to Haven Harbor, it's important to Mary."

"That would be great," said Mary. "I didn't know what to do with all these papers. Thank you so much for helping."

Mary and I had already made a major dent in the two cartons on the first floor.

Dave and Mary went upstairs to get the last carton, while Sarah and I began sorting the loose papers. Maybe the papers had been organized before—Mary'd said she'd found them in different places in the house, in drawers and desks and in the attic—but they weren't organized now.

I found three old deeds for Mary's house, showing how it had been transferred from one generation to another.

Sarah found a group of letters addressed to a Mary Clough from her husband, who was fighting in Europe in World War I.

"I'd love to read these," she said. "There's fascinating history here."

"Why don't you take them, then?" offered Mary, coming back into the room. "You're welcome to read them. But then I'd like them back."

"Of course," Sarah agreed, putting the packet of letters aside.

History as I remembered it from textbooks was a bore. Stories of people who'd lived a hundred years ago in the town you knew well . . . that was another story. I pulled an empty liquor box from the pile of empty cartons in the corner to hold the "Mary" papers.

It looked as though we'd all be there for a while.

Silence reigned. All I heard was the gentle turn of pages; of envelopes from the past being opened and scanned quickly. Occasionally someone would read a sentence out loud or check a date. The number of papers in the "Mary" box grew, but nothing we found was connected with the needlepoint.

"Here's something that might help," Dave said. "It's a page from a ship's log written by Captain Stephen Clough that shows his ship was in Le Havre in August of 1793. It doesn't list the contents of the ship, but that would have been the voyage that carried French furnishings home to Boston and Maine."

Mary nodded. "Wow! Now we know the legend of his being there was true."

"Although we don't know for sure what was on that ship," I cautioned. "Or who Captain Clough was working with."

"No. But August 1793 was during the Reign of Terror—when so many aristocrats and wealthy people were seized and guillotined without trials. Marie Antoinette was in the Bastille then. She was executed in October," Sarah pointed out.

"Not a good year for the ruling classes. I'd still like us to find an inventory of what was on that ship, and who it belonged to," I said, half joking. "Like, 'leather packet containing Mary Stuart embroidery to take home to wife.'"

"I don't think we're going to find anything

like that," said Sarah. "But at least now we have a ship leaving France and coming to the states at the time the clergy in Reims were hiding their valued artifacts. And we know Clough's friend James Swan knew Talleyrand, the archbishop in Reims, and Talleyrand knew Tronson du Coudray, Marie Antoinette's lawyer."

We kept looking. After a couple of hours Dave got up, stretched, and brought three beers and one soda (for Mary) from the kitchen.

The search went on.

Mary was the one who found it. "Here's a note signed by that Talleyrand person," she said. "It's in English, and it's faded. But—look!" she said, handing the note to me. "It's thanking Madame Clough for her hospitality, saying he admires her needlepoint, which he saw on his visit, and entrusting her with 'the enclosed treasure, stitched by a woman in distress.'"

"You're right, Mary. I think this is it." I passed the letter on to Sarah. "The 'enclosed treasure' must have been the embroidery. And the note is dated September of 1794. That's within the time period Ruth said Talleyrand visited Maine."

"Yeah!" Mary jumped up. "We have it! Imagine where that needlepoint has been, and who's touched it!"

"You have as close to provenance as we'll ever get," I said, happy for her, and relieved. "Now we just have to get the needlepoint back."

Chapter 36

May I with innocence and peace,
My fleeting moments spend;
And when this vale of life shall cease,
With calmness meet my end.

—Stitched by thirteen-year-old Sarah Ann
  Ewalt Patterson, Pittsburgh,
  Pennsylvania, 1819

We'd done as much as we could to identify
Mary's mysterious embroidery. She'd still have
to take it to a place like the Museum of Fine Arts
in Boston to have them look at it, but the provenance we'd uncovered—the possible, if not
certain, trail back to Mary, Queen of Scots—
would mean a lot.

And now Mary Clough was interested in the
history of her family. That was a real plus.

I thought about scheduling a day with Gram,
maybe next winter when Haven Harbor was

snowed or iced in, for her to tell me what she knew of our family. I knew a little. Now I'd like to know more.

When we left Mary last night she'd been bubbling about drawing a family tree, and she also wanted to frame the needlepoint.

When it was found.

As I straightened up my house and made toast for breakfast, I thought through what we knew.

Lenore Pendleton had opened the door of her house/office late at night.

Who would she open the door to at that time of night? Someone she knew. Most likely a woman. Or someone in distress, looking for help.

Okay. Whomever she let in convinced or forced her to open her safe. Then he or she hit her several times with a marble bookend that was on her desk, and left, taking with them no files, just jewelry and Mary's needlepoint.

Who would have known what she had in her safe? The only people who knew about the jewelry were her secretary, Glenda Pierce, her ex-husband, Charlie, and the sisters who were waiting for their mother's estate to be settled. They weren't even in Maine, so they weren't suspects. And Charlie was accounted for at the time Lenore was killed. That left Glenda.

Glenda was married and had a child. I could imagine Lenore opening the door to her secretary late at night. Especially if Glenda had a problem.

But why would Glenda have gone to see Lenore then? If she'd wanted to steal the jewelry she would have had opportunities during the day.

I couldn't rule Glenda out. But she was un-likely—and she hadn't known about the needle-point. On the other hand, maybe I should talk to her again.

So, who else had known the needlepoint might be valuable, and that it was in Lenore's safe?

Mary Clough, who had no reason to steal her own embroidery. Rob Trask. Uma Patel. But Rob seemed genuinely upset at finding Lenore's body, and thought of the needlepoint as his and Mary's to begin with. Uma? She wanted to see the needlepoint. She was ambitious. Was she cold enough to have agreed to go with Rob in the morning to see the needlepoint after she'd killed Lenore?

It would have made more sense if she'd seen the needlepoint first, and then killed to get it.

The police had considered her a prime sus-pect. But then where was the needlepoint? And why weren't her fingerprints on the bag of jew-elry in her luggage?

And why was she dead?

Could someone have killed her for the needlepoint and left the jewelry?

I frowned. Stranger things had happened.

I put that idea aside.

Who else knew about the needlepoint? Rob had told Arvin and Josh. Sarah and I had told Nicole Thibodeau. And, of course, Needlepoint-ers Sarah Byrne, Dave Percy, and Ruth Hopkins knew about it; they'd been at my home on the Fourth of July. And me.

I didn't take it. I grimaced to myself. One person to cross off my list. And maybe I was being prejudiced in favor of my friends, but I couldn't imagine Dave or Ruth killing Lenore. Ruth wouldn't have the physical strength. Dave would, and he did live across the street from Lenore. But no. I couldn't imagine Dave killing anyone. And if he had, he wouldn't have used a marble bookend. He had a garden full of poisons.

That left Nicole, who was exhausted from baking at the patisserie, and who'd told me she went to bed early. She needed money to take care of her mother-in-law. But kill Lenore?

Okay. That left Arvin and Josh. They were both young and strong. And at least a little drunk by the end of most evenings. Both were looking for money. Josh wanted to leave town, and Arvin wanted to buy a house and pay off the *Little Lady*. They'd both heard about the needle-point.

I added Jude and Cos to my list. Mary lived with the Currans. They would have known all about the needlepoint.

And of course Ethan, Rob's big brother and the homicide detective investigating, and his mother, also knew about the needlepoint. I almost laughed. No; I was sure Ethan and his mother were in the clear.

And then there was Uma's death. Somehow it was connected to Lenore's, since Lenore's jewelry was found in her room.

I needed to talk to Mrs. Clifford. And Glenda.
And Josh and Arvin. I reluctantly added Jude to
the list. She knew Josh, Arvin, and even Rob.
And she might know where they'd been when
Lenore was killed and Uma murdered.

Too many threads. Most of them leading
nowhere.

I'd come up with a couple of suspects for
Lenore's death. Uma's death was even more
troubling, because I couldn't think of a reason
for it, or a suspect. If someone was trying to
make people think Uma'd killed Lenore, why
hadn't that person just planted the jewelry in
her room? Why kill her?

And where was the needlepoint?

I felt surrounded by solid brick walls.

I wished Pete and Ethan had figured out who
killed Lenore. They'd had the crime scene
tested. They'd no doubt talked to everyone I'd
talked to, including all her neighbors. But if they
had any ideas or suspects, they hadn't shared
them.

I looked down at the paper I'd been doodling
on. I was definitely going to spend the day talking to people. I'd probably get a reputation for
being a busybody. But that was better than the
reputation I'd had when I was a teenager in town.

And I had a good reason to ask questions. I
was looking for a stolen needlepoint that we now
knew was valuable.

Who first?

I called Glenda.

Chapter 37

Every youth in the state, from the King's son downward, should learn to do something finely and thoroughly with his hands.

—John Ruskin (1819–1900),
   English art critic, in "Letter XXI,
   Of the Dignity of the Four Fine Arts,"
   April 15, 1867, published in Fors
   Clavigera (1871–1884)

Glenda told me she'd be at Lenore's office all day.

"Sure, you can stop in, Angie. Is it about your appointment to make out your will? I'm in the middle of making out a list of other lawyers nearby who've agreed to pick up Lenore's clients."

"I wanted to talk to you for a few minutes about Lenore. Making out my will isn't an emergency." At least I certainly hoped it wasn't.

"I'll be here all day," Glenda answered. "I'm not sure I'll be able to help you, but I'd be glad to try."

I started to walk in the direction of the law offices when I turned around. Glenda was cleaning and organizing Lenore's office. I was asking a favor that would take time away from that. I decided to bring her a box of pastries. If she didn't want them now, she could take them home with her.

I was becoming Nicole's best customer. I felt as though I'd been in her patisserie every day of the past week.

For good reasons, of course.

I must have missed the morning rush for pastries and bread. Only one man was ahead of me, and he ordered one cheese Danish. Not a complicated order.

But the Danish pastries did look good. I ordered five assorted. I'd eat one myself and give the other four to Glenda.

"So, have you found that needlepoint yet?" Nicole asked as she added up my order.

"No. But we think we may have figured out its provenance," I said.

"Does that mean it's worth a lot of money?"

"It might," I said. "The next step should be to show the embroidery to an expert at a museum who knows antique needlework. We're just learning."

"But this valuable needlepoint is gone," she said.

I shrugged. "I hope not. I hope we can find it."

"And find out who killed that lawyer, Mrs. Pendleton."

"Exactly." I took the box she handed me. "How is Henri's mother?"

"A little better, thank you. We have no answers yet."

"I wish you well," I said. I could read the frustration on Nicole's face.

"*Merci*. Thank you for asking," she said. "We do have help. Old friends from home have been visiting. We've told them our problems. They've promised to look in on Henri's mother back in Quebec. It will help to have someone else visiting her when we cannot."

I nodded.

As we were talking a family of five came into the patisserie and began debating which pastries each would choose.

I headed for Lenore Pendleton's office, nibbling my treat along the way.

The wind was gusty, and gray clouds were low, threatening rain. I walked quickly. If it rained, and I got wet, I'd dry. Soggy pastries would not. I should have paid closer attention to the weather forecast.

The door to Lenore's house and office was open, as usual during business hours. Was it only a week ago I'd brought the needlepoint to her so it would be safe? So much had happened since then.

The office that had seemed so clean and organized and friendly was now full of cartons full of client files or law books. Glenda had cleaned off Lenore's desk and was sorting papers there.

A marble bookend was leaning against a pile of books now on the floor. The matching bookend must have been the murder weapon. The police would have taken it so the crime lab could check for fingerprints.

"Hi, Glenda," I said. "Thanks for agreeing to see me." I held up the box. "I brought you some pastries."

"Thank you!" she said. "Would you mind putting them in the kitchen? It's through that door, to the right," she said, pointing. "They'll be a treat for lunch."

Lenore's kitchen felt empty, perhaps because it was so neat.

Glenda followed me in. "Put the box on the counter by the sink," she said.

I did, and she peeked in. "Oooh. I love Danish pastries." Then she looked at me and her eyes welled up. "So did Lenore. She bought us pastries as a treat after we'd had a rough week, or after one of her cases was settled. She had some right here in her kitchen, sitting on the table, the night she died."

"I'm sorry. I didn't mean to bring back memories," I said. I should have chosen something other than Danish.

"No, no. You wouldn't have known. I saw a box like this here last week, when I was making out that inventory for the police. I was glad. She'd had her favorite treats that last night."

"I guess they were left from the afternoon," I said.

"I don't think so. When I stopped in that afternoon she told me she hadn't left her office all day," Glenda said. "She must have bought them after work."

I looked at the pastry box. "You were here that day?"

"Only briefly," Glenda said. "I had errands to do in town, so I stopped in about four in the afternoon with Tyler to pick up a couple of books Lenore'd loaned me. We both enjoyed mysteries, especially those set in Maine. She kept a stack of them for us to read at home, or during quiet days at the office. I decided to take a couple home to read during my vacation week. I picked out books by Kaitlyn Dunnett, Barbara Ross, and Jim Hayman."

"And Lenore was here then? At four o'clock?"

"She was on the telephone. I waved at her and held up the books so she'd know why I'd stopped in. I got Tyler a drink of water in the kitchen, and then I left."

"Are you sure there weren't any pastries here then?"

Glenda looked at me strangely. "I don't remember any. But I wasn't looking for them."

When did the patisserie close in the afternoon? That wouldn't be hard to find out. The hours were probably even listed on their Web site.

So Lenore had been alive at four in the afternoon. That wasn't a surprise. Ethan had said she was killed at eleven or twelve o'clock that night.

Plenty of time to close up her office, buy pastries, and come back. She'd probably eaten dinner and then gotten ready for bed before her late night caller arrived.

"Have you thought of anyone she might have opened her door to?" I asked Glenda.

"No one," she said. "Or—anyone in town. She knew everyone. But only a few people knew about her safe, or that she kept jewelry in it." She paused. "Whoever it was must just have wanted what was in there. Lenore's pocketbook was in the kitchen, and none of her money or credit cards were missing. And our petty cash was left in my top desk drawer. I've wondered why they didn't take our computers." She pointed at the ceiling. "Lenore had more electronics and her good silver in her private rooms, upstairs, but none of those things were touched so far as the police could tell. They asked me to check, but I didn't notice anything missing either." Glenda stood and looked around. "Why would anyone kill Lenore? I don't know. It was only jewelry. It wasn't worth her life."

That was the question all of us had been struggling with.

Chapter 38

Perhaps there is no single influence which has had more salutary effects in promising the comforts of home and the respectability of family life throughout the lengths and breadth of our land, than the attention given in our own Magazine to illustrations and directions which make needlework and fancy works in all their varieties known and accessible. Home is the place for such pursuits; by encouraging these, we make women happier and men better.

—From *Godey's Lady's Book and Magazine,*
   January 1864

Next stop: talk to Mary, and maybe Cos and Jude.

Cos and Mary were having lunch together when I got to the Currans' house. They seemed to do that every day. "Where's Jude?" I asked, looking around. Usually all three girls were there.

"She's at Maine Waves," said Cos. "Last winter she worked only three days a week, because she was the newest hairdresser there, but now it's summer and a lot more people are in town, so she's working five days a week. And two nights." Cos shook her head. "I want to go to college next year. Become a nurse or a midwife. I want to make a difference. Jude says hairdressers make a difference. They help people look their best. But I wouldn't want to spend the rest of my life shampooing and cutting hair."

"Sounds like you have big plans for your future," I said. "Best of luck!"

"I haven't worked it all out yet. I have to decide what schools to apply to·this fall. And I have another year in high school." She grinned. "Seniors rule the school!"

"So I've heard."

"I wish Mary would postpone her wedding so she'd be in school with me this year." She looked pointedly at Mary, who was mixing tuna fish salad. "School won't be the same without her. And she's going to miss the senior pep rally, and the senior prom. Mom and Dad told her she's welcome to stay here. They're not throwing her out when she's eighteen." She paused. "Her grades are higher than mine. We'd always planned to room together at college. Now she'll be here in Haven Harbor, probably having a baby or something, and I'll have to go to college alone."

"Stop hassling me, Cos. You don't have to go to college," said Mary. "You can stay here and get a job, like I'm going to do."

Cos shook her head. "I'm not staying here just

because you and Jude are here. I don't want to
be like Jude. And what job can you get without
even a high school diploma? Being a supermar-
ket clerk or a chambermaid?"

"Jude's doing all right. She went to cosmetol-
ogy school and got her fifteen hundred hours in
and her license. She's only twenty, and she's got
a solid job. That sounds good to me," said Mary.
"I'll find a job. I'm not the career type. I want to
settle down and have a family."

"Just because Jude has a job here now doesn't
mean she's going to stay," said Cos. "She says she
could get a job doing hair anywhere in the country. All she has to do is get licensed in a new
state, and she says that won't be hard. She keeps
saying she's going to leave, soon. Go where
there's more excitement than in Haven Harbor."

I'd headed west as soon as I'd graduated. Who
was I to say Jude was wrong? Proving you could
make it by yourself, without the security of friends
and family near at hand, was part of growing up.
"Where's Jude talking about going?" I asked.

"I don't know. Maybe Florida. She says Maine
only has two seasons—July and winter. And she's
tired of winter."

"Well, I'm happy right here in Haven Harbor,
and I'm getting married and staying," said Mary
decisively. "Jude can go to Florida, and you can
go off to college. I bet you'll both be back. You
have family here."

"Everyone has to make their own choices," I
said. I'd graduated from high school before I'd
left Maine, like Jude had and Cos was planning
to do. I wished Mary would get her diploma

before her marriage license. But when you're young you want to do everything now. I'd been pretty darn good at ignoring advice when I'd been her age. "What about Jude and Josh? The other night he told me he wanted to leave town. Do you think they'll go together?" I asked.

Mary and Cos exchanged glances.

"Josh is a total pain," Mary said. "He has lots of big ideas, but he doesn't follow through. Half the time he and Jude plan to get together he stands her up."

"And he tries to make it with every girl in town," said Cos, rubbing her rear end. "I swear, I get bruises just looking at that idiot."

I tried not to laugh. "So you're saying Josh isn't as devoted to Jude as she hopes."

"No way," said Mary. "She's dreaming if she thinks he's going to take her away from Haven Harbor so they can live happily ever after."

"I think she's beginning to see that," Cos added, putting lunch plates on the table for all three of us. Mary'd made me a tuna sandwich, too. "I heard them arguing the other night."

"When was that?" I asked.

She thought a minute. "The night after the fireworks. Wednesday night." The night Sarah and I'd seen Josh and Jude at the co-op with Arvin and Rob.

"It was late. After midnight."

And the night Lenore was killed—close to midnight.

"What were they arguing about?" I asked as Mary put sandwiches on our plates and poured us each glasses of milk. I hadn't had a glass of milk in a long time. But I didn't mention that.

"I couldn't understand them," said Cos. "They were outside. But they were definitely having a fight. I don't know if they've even seen each other since then."

Mary shook her head. "You're right. Those three guys—Arvin and Rob and Josh—used to be like the Three Musketeers. Out together almost every night. Jude usually went with them."

"You didn't join them?" I asked.

"All they do is drink beer. I'm not old enough to drink in a bar. And I don't like the taste or smell of beer anyway," said Mary. "In the winter I had homework, and now I have my house to clear out. I don't mind staying home. Jude likes going out."

"Especially since Josh got back to town," Cos put in.

"But something must have happened last week. Because Rob hasn't even been talking much to me," added Mary. "He's been hanging around with his brother, which isn't usual, even when Ethan's in town."

I'd seen Josh alone at the Harbor Haunts a few nights before.

The girls were right. Something was different.

What had that argument been about last Wednesday night after midnight?

Chapter 39

Mourn, Hapless Brethren Deeply Mourn
The Source of Every Joy is Fled
Our Father Dear The Friend of Man
The Godlike Washington is Dead.

—Stitched by Eliza Thomas, Media,
 Pennsylvania, 1804. George Washington
 was sixty-seven when he died in 1799
 at his home in Mount Vernon, Virginia.

I was convinced neither Mary nor Cos knew anything that would either help find the missing needlepoint or solve the two murders.

It was beginning to rain when I left the Currans' house.

Where to next? The Wild Rose Inn was farther away than the harbor. I decided to dodge raindrops and head downtown.

The light rain had driven most waterfront visitors indoors. Even the ice-cream store was full of people slurping cones and looking out the window, waiting for the rain to stop.

I glanced at my phone. It was a little past two.

If Arvin had gone lobstering this morning at five, the usual time to get out on the water, he should be returning about now.

I checked the town pier. His *Little Lady* was there, but his morning's catch wasn't on board, and the deck had been swabbed. Lobstering wasn't a romantic occupation, despite all the cute plush stuffed lobsters for sale in local gift shops. Lobstering was smelly and messy.

Arvin had sold his catch and cleaned up for the day.

I wiped the rain off my face and walked down to the co-op. Lobstermen (and women) often gathered in the office and lobster pound. It was a good guess Arvin was there now.

And he was, talking to Josh. They'd both been on my list. This was a twofer.

"Finished for the day?" I asked, interrupting whatever they'd been talking about.

"Yup. You looking to buy lobsters?" Arvin asked. The large open tanks were in back of him; pound and pound and a quarters in one, pound and a halves in another, and the largest lobsters in the third. Lobsters under one pound or over four pounds had to be thrown back. Lobsters sold by the pound. A price list, changed daily, was on a blackboard near the tanks.

"Not today," I said.

"Then what're you doing here?" asked Josh. "Mom said you were over to our house the other day, asking about me. Checking up on me?"

"Why would I be checking up on you? I'm just trying to figure out what happened to Mary Clough's needlepoint," I said.

"You think it's here?" he said skeptically. "In the co-op pound?"

"I wondered if you or Arvin knew anything about it. Or about Uma Patel's death."

"Listen, I've already talked to the police," said Arvin. "She said she'd never been lobstering, so I invited her out. I hauled a couple of traps. Then I brought her back to the dock. I don't know what happened to her after that."

"I know what Alice said about that," said Josh, grinning. "She wasn't exactly thrilled to hear you'd taken that girl out for a boat ride. The way I heard it, she was ready to take your kid and go home to her mother after the police called looking for you."

"Alice doesn't know what she's talking about," said Arvin. "I offered the girl a free boat ride. I was being nice to a tourist."

"A wicked pretty one," added Josh.

"I heard the medical examiner said she'd hit her head pretty hard on something," I said. "Do you know anything about that?"

Arvin ran his fingers, wet with sea water, through his hair. "She was alive when she left my boat. No one asked me about a bump on her head."

"What happened?" I asked.

"The deck of my boat's pretty slippery," he said defensively. "I'd cleaned it after the morning's haul, but she was dumb enough to come on board wearing leather sandals."

True enough. Lobster boat decks would be wet with ocean water, pieces of bait, bits of seaweed, and various flotsam and jetsam brought up with the traps. Decks were cleaned after every trip. Lobstermen were proud of their boats. A boat was an investment, an office, and a future. But no one who knew anything about boats would go on board without wearing rubber-soled shoes.

"So she slipped?"

Arvin shuffled his feet and glanced around, as though he didn't want anyone to overhear him. "I was handing her a life jacket, and she slipped on the deck. Hit her head on the railing. But I helped her up, and she seemed fine. No blood, and she laughed about it. I don't know what happened to her after she left the *Little Lady*. But she was fine when she walked up the ramp."

"Did you tell Ethan Trask that?" I asked.

"Not at first. I didn't know it was important. But, yeah, when he called me again last night I told him." He looked at me. "I wouldn't lie about a thing like that. Plenty of people must have seen that girl after she left my boat." He looked straight at me. "And, no. She wasn't wearing any fancy necklace when she was on my boat. She wasn't wearing any necklace at all." He almost looked contrite. "I'm sure about that because her T-shirt was . . . low in front. I noticed that. I didn't tell the police that right away because I figured the way this town is, it would get back to Alice."

"You're in trouble." Josh teased. "The police

better find people who saw Uma after she left you. If no one saw her, you've got a big problem."

"She was fine," Arvin repeated. "Fine. Sure, maybe she had a bruise. But no way was she dead that afternoon." He looked at me "And she wasn't wearing any fancy necklace, and she didn't have any embroidery or bags of jewelry with her. She was just a girl in shorts and sandals and a T-shirt. I don't know what happened to her after that."

Of course, he did know. We all did.

Uma Patel had died.

Chapter 40

Say, while you press with growing love,
The darling to your heart,
And all a mother's pleasures prove,
Are you entirely blest?
But every pain the infant feels,
The mother feels it too!
Then wispers busy cruel fear
The child, alas, may die
And nature prompts the ready tear
And heaves the rising sigh.

—Stitched by twelve-year-old
Hetty Muhlenberg,
Reading, Pennsylvania, 1797

The rain had stopped, but the day was still dank
and overcast. I shivered as I walked up the hill
from the wharves to my house.

Once, when I was little, it had started to rain

on a sunny July day, ruining our chances for a
promised picnic. Mama had taken my hand and
pulled me outside anyway. We'd danced with
the raindrops. I had a sudden memory of the
double rainbow that appeared over the harbor
that day.

I'd never minded rain after that. To prove it,
I stomped through a couple of puddles on my
way home. "In your honor, Mama," I said to
myself.

Uma had slipped and fallen on Arvin's boat.
That explained one of the bruises or blows the
ME had identified.

But Ethan had said she'd "been hit" several
times.

Could she and Arvin have underestimated
how hard she'd hit the deck? Sports commenta-
tors talked about football and soccer players
who'd had concussions that didn't show up immediately. Maybe after her lobstering adventure
she'd gone for a walk on the rocks and gotten
dizzy, or slipped and fallen again. If she was still
wearing leather sandals, that wouldn't be sur-
prising.

Her feet were bare when I found her body
tangled in seaweed.

Tides could have washed shoes away.

And tides could have dashed her body on the
rocks. Despite what the ME had said, that might
explain the other marks on her body.

I hoped so.

Maybe no one had killed Uma. Maybe she'd
been the victim of carelessness and ignorance of
the dangers of the Maine coast.

But the ME had said she was dead before she was in the water.

Dead people didn't bleed. Or bruise.

And my theory didn't explain how a stolen sapphire necklace had gotten around her neck.

Assuming I believed Arvin's story, whatever happened to Uma had happened after she left the *Little Lady*.

At home, I changed out of my wet clothes. Dancing in the rain had been fun when I was five. Walking around town in wet jeans and a sweatshirt wasn't comfortable.

I still had time to visit the Wild Rose Inn. I'd put off that trip. Tom had arranged for Uma's parents to stay at the inn, and I didn't want to run into them. They deserved their privacy.

Mrs. Clifford was at the front desk when I got to the Wild Rose. No one else was in the small lobby. "I'm sorry, no press," she said without looking up. Then she recognized me. "Oh. You're not press. You're the young woman who came to see Uma Patel last week, aren't you? I'm sorry—almost everyone who's opened that door today has been from the media." She shook her head. "I wish they'd leave that poor girl's family alone."

"I'm sorry to bother you," I said. "This must be an awful time."

She nodded. "At first a couple of my other guests stayed around, to see what all the excitement was about. But then the police starting searching rooms, and the Patels arrived." She shuddered. "And the press. It's been awful. Now everyone's checked out except the Patels. I've told them they can have all their meals here. I don't usually offer my guests anything more than breakfast, but how could they go out anywhere when people are always asking them questions? Such a tragedy. And then the police found that jewelry in their daughter's room." She shook her head. "I don't know what to think. She certainly didn't seem like a murderer or thief to me."

"So no one else is here now?"

"Just the Patels. And I had a full inn. All eight rooms were reserved for the first two weeks in July. I was straight out, arranging hair and massage appointments for the guests, and boat rides and fishing trips. Now—nothing."

I remembered the couple who'd been sitting at the same breakfast table as Uma. And the Nolins, those art and antiques dealers from Quebec. And there'd been five other full rooms? I glanced around. The inn was deserted.

"I liked Uma," I said. "I agree with you. I can't believe she'd have killed Lenore Pendleton. Someone must have put that jewelry in her room." And around her neck, I added to myself.

Mrs. Clifford looked perplexed. "I have no idea how. I have a key that opens all the doors, and of course the maid does. But I can't believe anyone who works for me would have done such a thing."

"Did Uma have any visitors when she was here?"

"You, of course," said Mrs. Clifford. "I don't remember anyone else. The police asked me when she got in at night, and whether she had any company. But I don't keep track of my guests.

Unless I'm down here in the lobby by chance, I don't know when they come or go."

She sighed. "We've never had any problems like this. That girl could have had a friend visit, or someone could have met her here. I just don't know."

"I understand," I said. "But thank you."

"I don't know what to think," said Mrs. Clifford. "Things like this don't happen in Haven Harbor."

I nodded and left.

Mrs. Clifford was wrong.

Things like that did happen in Haven Harbor. They'd happened to my mother. And to Lenore Pendleton.

And to Uma Patel.

Chapter 41

Oh woman, in thy idleness thou has sought out many inventions, besides making pin-cushions, working worsted, and getting up fairs for everything conceivable. But industry is better than idleness, however frivolous the industry may be.

—Miss Mary Orme, *Godey's Magazine and Lady's Book*, 1846

My kitchen calendar told me it was July, but the house seemed damp after the drenching rain.

I'd spent the day talking to people about what had happened to Uma and Lenore, and I hadn't learned anything. Or gotten any closer to finding Mary's needlepoint.

I curled up on the living room couch with a cup of cocoa and turned on the television. Three people I didn't care about were earnestly answering questions about the War of the Roses on *Jeopardy*.

English history. What did it matter that we might have figured out the history of a piece of needlepoint, if now the needlepoint had disappeared and two people were dead?

I'd about decided to add marshmallows, and maybe brandy, to my cocoa, when my phone started vibrating. I'd forgotten to turn the ringer on after talking to people this afternoon.

It was Mary Clough.

I almost didn't pick up her call. I didn't have any news for Mary, and certainly no good news. I sighed and pushed the button.

"Angie, I need help." Mary's voice was low and scared. "It's Jude. I don't know what to do."

I sat upright and muted the television. "What about Jude?"

"Jude and Cos and I share a room," said Mary, her voice still quiet. "I just went to borrow Jude's yellow hoodie. She lets me."

"Yes?" What was scary about borrowing a sweatshirt?

"I found it, in her bottom drawer, in the corner, under her sweaters."

"You found her sweatshirt?"

"No! You don't understand! I'm pretty sure it's Mrs. Pendleton's ring. The emerald one that was stolen." She paused. "I saw her wearing it once. I told her I liked it, and she took it off and showed it to me. Said it had belonged to her grandmother. And there's a gun in the drawer, too."

"Does Jude shoot?" I was trying to stay cool, and calm Mary. Lots of Mainers had guns. By itself, that might not be a problem.

"I've never heard her talk about shooting. Or

hunting. And the gun's a little one. The kind people carry. Not the kind they use for hunting." Mary paused, as if to take a deep breath. "It wasn't there the last time I opened that drawer, I'm sure. Angie, I'm scared."

Lenore's emerald cocktail ring hadn't been with the stolen jewelry found in Uma's suitcase at the Wild Rose.

"Where's Jude now?"

"Downstairs, watching television with Cos."

"Don't say anything to her," I cautioned. "Maybe there's an explanation."

"Not a good one," said Mary. "There can't be!"

"We don't know for sure. Mary, you have to stay calm. Don't tell anyone you called me. I'm going to come over. I'll talk to Jude."

"Can you come soon? Please?"

"Right away," I promised.

Where could Jude have gotten that ring? I wasn't happy about a gun showing up in her room, but it wasn't hard to get a gun in Maine. Jude was twenty. Lots of Mainers her age had guns. But if Mary hadn't seen a gun during the two years she'd lived with the Currans, then chances are it was new.

Why would Jude need a gun?

I hoped there'd be a reasonable explanation. Maybe it was for protection, because of Lenore's and Uma's deaths. Maybe someone gave her both the ring and the gun. But if that was Lenore's ring, she had stolen property. And whoever gave it to her might have been the one who stole it. And killed Lenore.

This situation could get messy. Fast.

I wasn't stupid. Mary might have called me, but the police needed to know what was happening.

I pressed Ethan's number on my cell. "Mary Clough just called me. She saw an emerald ring in one of Jude Curran's drawers. She thinks it was Lenore's. Plus, she saw a gun in the drawer. She said it was small; I'm assuming it was a handgun."

"Jude Curran? What has she got to do with all this? And where in hell did she get that ring?" Ethan sounded distracted. Not happy I'd called.

"I don't know. I don't think she got the ring or gun at Maine Waves. But I'm hoping she'll talk to me about it." I paused. "She's sweet on Josh Winslow. He could be involved."

Ethan was silent. "I should go with you, Angie."

"Let me try first. If I didn't think you should be involved I wouldn't have called you," I pointed out. "Jude might talk to another woman more than to a state trooper. Especially if she's covering for Josh."

"We don't know for sure that ring was Lenore's," Ethan pointed out.

"No. But Mary thought she recognized it. And how many people in Haven Harbor have emerald rings? I don't think a hairdresser just out of school could afford one."

"Okay. You go talk to Jude. But I'm going to the Currans' house, too. It'll take me a couple of minutes; I have to get Emmie out of the bathtub. But I'll be there. I'll park close by, down the street. If you have any problems, call me. You don't have to leave a message. I'll come right away."

"I will. I promise."

I hesitated a moment, then pulled off my sweatshirt, slipped my gun into my shoulder holster, and pulled the sweatshirt back on. I checked my mirror. Yes, the gun was now concealed, and no, my Maine concealed carry permit hadn't come through yet. I hadn't been back in Maine for the full six months' waiting period. But in case of trouble I'd rather be armed than legal.

I left my angel necklace on. It wouldn't hurt to have a little extra luck tonight.

I drove to the Currans' small tan house. It was faster than walking.

Getting out I smelled freshly cut grass. Daisies were blooming around the "Curran" mailbox. Just a quiet evening in a scenic coastal village. I hoped.

I looked around. When I didn't see Ethan's car I waited a few seconds. But he'd promised. He should be here any minute.

Cos came to the door after I rang.

"Angie! We didn't expect you." She opened the door for me to come in.

The television in the living room was on, just as Mary had said. They were watching some survival reality show.

"Hi, Angie," said Mary, joining Cos at the door. "Good to see you."

I touched her shoulder to let her know she'd done the right thing. Where was Jude? "Are your parents home, Cos?" I asked.

If they were, I'd want them to know I was there.

"Mom went grocery shopping and Dad's next door watching the Sox game."

"And Jude?" I asked. I glanced around. She wasn't in the living room.

"I'm here," she said, coming down the stairs. She had a full backpack slung over one shoulder and was wearing a long, loose top over her jeans. Did she have a holster for her gun? Mary'd said the gun was small. That top could hide a gun.

I knew. Mine did.

"Could I talk with you for a few minutes, Jude?" I asked.

"What about?" she said. "If you want your hair done you can come to the salon. I'm on my own time now. I was about to leave."

She continued toward the door.

"Just a few minutes," I said. "The rain's stopped. We could talk outside in the yard." I wanted to get her away from the other two girls. And, if possible, in Ethan's sight. I didn't have a good feeling about what might happen next.

She frowned. "Only for a minute. I have to go."

I followed her out the door.

She turned to me. "Okay. What do you want?"

I decided to be blunt. "Where did you get the emerald ring, Jude?"

"What emerald ring?" She backed up a couple of steps.

"The one in the drawer with your sweatshirts and sweaters."

"How do you . . ." She went toward the door,

and yelled in, "You little bitch! You went through my things and then told?"

I put my hand out to stop her. "Mary was worried about you, Jude."

"It's none of her business what I do. None of yours, either," said Jude. "That ring is mine."

"Where did you get it?" I asked.

"I don't have to say," she answered.

"Is it Lenore Pendleton's ring?" I asked. "If it is, you should tell me how you got it, because it was stolen. You're in real trouble for having it."

She stood on the grass, crossing her arms in front of her chest. She didn't say anything. She just glared at me.

"Who gave it to you, Jude? If you tell me, and I tell the police, you won't be in as much trouble."

"I'm not talking," she said. "That ring is mine, and I'm keeping it. I deserve it. I've wasted too much of my life in this boring town already, always doing what other people want me to do. It's time for me to do what I want."

I heard a car pull up and stop. I didn't turn. Would Ethan park so close?

Jude glanced in back of me as we heard the car door open.

"Josh! Hold on. I'm coming." She ran past me down the brick path to the car. As she did she yelled to him, "Angie knows about the ring. She's gonna blab."

I ran after her. "Jude, wait! You'll be in more trouble than you are now if you don't talk to me."

Josh hadn't said a word, but he'd gotten back in the car. He reached to open the passenger seat door for Jude. She jumped in and slammed the door before I got to the car window.

"Stop, Jude! Don't make this worse!"

"You don't understand! You don't know anything!" she yelled through the open window. "Just leave us alone. Stay away!" As she spoke she pulled her gun out from beneath her shirt and pointed it at me.

I stopped. Everything seemed to be in slow motion. I backed up, and reached for my weapon.

I'd just pulled it out when Josh gunned his car.

He sideswiped a parked car ahead of him, making a horrible scraping sound as he swerved into the middle of the narrow residential street.

He didn't stop.

Before I had a chance to react Ethan's car passed me, in pursuit of Jude and Josh.

I raced to my car, jumped in, and tried to follow them.

But they both had a head start.

Chapter 42

Come now let us forget our mirth
And think that we must die
What are our best delights on earth
Compared with those on high.

—Stitched by Sally C. Lovejoy,
age ten, 1811

Josh's car wove in and around the narrow village streets.

Ethan was on his tail, siren blaring. I tried to keep up.

Other cars, drivers out for a quiet evening, pulled as far as they could to the side of the road.

Josh drove through two red lights, swerving around other cars.

He didn't slow down.

Within a few minutes we were all out on Route 1, heading north on the two-lane road.

Josh veered from one side of his lane to the other, passing cars to his right and his left.

My hands clutched my steering wheel. Why was I following them both? But I'd gotten this far. I needed to know how it would end.

I drove faster than I ever had before. But I couldn't keep up with the others. Every moment, I imagined one or all three of us crashing.

My stomach muscles lurched as trucks and cars going both north and south pulled over onto the shoulder, trying to get out of our way.

One car hit a ditch. It teetered precariously on its side before falling back onto its wheels.

Josh put his hand on his horn and held it there.

One pickup he narrowly missed ended up in a ditch, trying to get out of his way. As I passed it I hoped no one inside had been hurt.

I hoped Ethan had somehow called the guys at the local police station.

As our speed increased, and the road became curvier, the chances of the chase ending well dropped.

I almost pulled over, following the lead of other cars on the road. But my foot stayed on the accelerator.

The sun was going down. It was harder to see in the dark. I switched on my lights, focused on the road, and accelerated again.

Neither Josh nor Ethan had turned on their

lights. They were driving close to ninety. Maybe faster. I didn't take my eyes off the road to look at the speedometer.

Even on this relatively straight stretch of Route 1, we were going way past the speed limit.

Way too fast

Suddenly Josh braked. His car fishtailed into the southbound lane where an RV was trying to get to the side of the road, out of his way.

That driver wasn't fast enough. The RV was wide and long. Josh and Jude crashed against its side, leaving the RV on its side off the road, caught between two trees.

Ethan braked in response. His car skidded sideways, coming to a halt across both lanes of traffic. I stomped on my brakes and barely missed hitting Ethan's car as my tires screeched in protest.

I sat, frozen, my car still shaking, as I tried to figure out what had happened.

I turned off my engine.

Ahead of us my headlights showed a small brown and white dog barking loudly and running back and forth from one side of the road to the other.

That's why Josh put on his brakes. To avoid hitting the dog.

I got out and ran to the other vehicles. Ethan was standing near where Josh's car had smashed into the RV. He was calling the scene in.

The driver of the RV was carefully crawling

out of his vehicle. He looked shaken but intact. His RV wasn't.

The front of Josh's car was smashed in.

Josh and Jude were both trapped in the car.

I couldn't see either of them behind the torn, crumpled metal that had been their car.

Slivers of glass shone in the long grasses by the side of the road, caught by the RV's headlights.

Chapter 43

When I am dead and in my grave
And all my bones are rotten,
When this you see, remember me
That I may not be forgotten.

—Stitched by Polly Young,
age eleven, 1801

The next half hour was a blur.

The fire and police departments and ambulance arrived. They had to cut Josh and Jude out of their car. By some miracle, both of them were alive, but unconscious and covered with blood. They were airlifted to Maine Medical in Portland.

I heard later that Jude's back was badly bruised, her face was cut, she'd lost several teeth, one of her arms was shattered, and both her ankles were broken.

Josh wasn't as lucky. He hadn't made it.

Ethan said he was fine. My chest was bruised by my seat belt, but that was minor.

In the luggage compartment of Josh's car the police found a duffel bag containing twenty-five thousand dollars and Josh's clothing.

He and Jude had been planning to leave Maine that night and head south.

Lenore Pendleton's emerald ring was in Jude's backpack, along with all her savings. She'd withdrawn it from the bank earlier that day.

No one knew the whole story until Jude was well enough to answer questions and her parents convinced her to cooperate.

It seemed she and Josh had heard from Rob and Mary how valuable Mary's needlepoint might be. After a few too many beers, Jude and Josh had gone to Lenore's house Wednesday night to convince her to open her safe. When Lenore hadn't agreed at once, they'd threatened her.

Then, after she'd opened the safe, Josh had killed her out of fear she'd identify them. It had been on impulse. Killing hadn't been in their plan.

They'd taken the needlepoint and the jewelry.

Then they'd panicked. What should they do? Who would buy stolen goods?

Neither of them had planned their next steps.

But they'd remembered Rob talking to Uma, and then to the Nolins, about the needlepoint.

Their goal was to make enough money to leave Haven Harbor. Jude called Mrs. Nolin, whose hair she'd cut at Maine Waves. She agreed to sell the Nolins the needlepoint if they'd get rid of the jewelry by putting it in Uma's room at the inn.

They kept out the sapphire necklace, to tie Uma to the crime, and the emerald ring, because Jude wanted it.

After Uma was back from lobstering with Arvin, Josh had followed her to the ledges by the lighthouse and hit her with a rock. Before he pushed her body into the water he'd fastened the sapphire necklace around her neck. He and Jude assumed Uma would be blamed for Lenore's death, especially since the Nolins agreed to plant the jewelry in Uma's room using her key, which Josh had taken.

They'd paid Josh and Jude twenty-five thousand dollars for the needlepoint and headed home to Quebec.

The needlepoint might have been worth more if they'd had the provenance we'd been working so hard to provide, but under the circumstances, they weren't picky.

The Canadian police had no trouble finding them. Or the stolen embroidery.

Mary would be getting her needlepoint back—after Jude's trial.

Chapter 44

Teach me to feel another's woe
To hide the fault I see
That mercy I to others shew
That mercy shew to me.

—Stitched by Susanna Magarge
at the Quaker School,
Bristol, Pennsylvania, 1827

Rev. Tom's sermon on the Sunday after that was on forgiveness.

I wondered how Uma's family felt. They weren't in church, of course. They'd taken their daughter's body back to Connecticut.

I wasn't as worried about Lenore's ex. Although I was surprised to see Charlie slide into a back pew after the first hymn.

Maybe he had things to think about. And maybe he'd even get his jewelry back. I didn't know what Lenore's will had said.

It didn't seem important anymore.

Mary and Rob were there, holding hands. I hoped the events of the past week would pull them closer together.

I was most worried about two people who weren't in church: Ob and Anna Winslow. They'd spent the past week sequestered at home, trying to deal with the loss of their son.

I hoped they'd be ready to talk soon. Josh's funeral was scheduled for Tuesday.

What Josh had done wasn't his parents' fault, but I knew how Haven Harbor reacted when one of their own made a mistake. Forgiveness might sound good on Sunday morning, but it would take a while for the community to absorb what had happened.

Jude's family wasn't in church either.

But the town would heal. I knew that, too, from personal experience.

After all, I was here.

Haven Harbor had accepted me back. I was settling in, making myself at home.

I even had plans. I'd started making new lists.

First, I'd contact interior decorators in Portsmouth and Boston about Mainely Needlepoint's services.

Second, the kitchen could use a coat of paint.

After that, I vowed to ask Gram to teach me to make blueberry muffins.

And to show me how to do more needlepoint stitches.

I might even get a cat.

I was going to be all right.

And Haven Harbor would go on.

Angie Curtis's Strawberry-Rhubarb Pie

❧ Classic June/July Maine Dessert ❧

Ingredients

- 2 frozen 9-inch deep-dish pie shells
  (Angie's never learned to make pie crust;
  if you have, make your own!)
- 2½ cups fresh rhubarb, cut in ½- to 1-inch
  pieces
- 2½ cups fresh strawberries, stems removed
  and cut in half
- ⅓ cup flour
- 1⅓ cups granulated sugar plus a little to
  sprinkle on top
- 2 tablespoons cinnamon
- 1 tablespoon lemon juice
- 3 tablespoons salted butter, cut in small
  pieces

Heat oven to 425 degrees. Remove pie shells from freezer.

Mix flour, sugar, and cinnamon in large bowl.

Add lemon juice and cut-up rhubarb and strawberries. Mix together lightly—with hands is usually best.

Put everything inside one of the pie shells. Dot top of fruit with small pieces of butter.

Cover with second pie shell, squeezing edges together. Cut several slits in the top shell and sprinkle with sugar.

Place on rimmed baking sheet (to catch juices that will escape from the pie while it is cooking) and place in center of oven about 45 minutes, or until juices bubble and crust is browned.

May be served warm or cold. Top with vanilla ice cream for an extra treat.

Variations

Use blueberries instead of strawberries. Use both blueberries and strawberries. Use small pieces of pear or apple instead of berries.

Author's Notes

Of course, *Thread and Gone* is fiction. So far as I know no pieces of embroidery stitched by Mary, Queen of Scots, have been found in Maine attics. Although you never know what might turn up in the future!

It is true that Mary Stuart, her cousin Elizabeth I of England, and two hundred years later, Marie Antoinette, were all needlepointers.

And although this story is fictional, certainly Mary's life, and those of the "four Marys" who attended her, including Mary Seton, were real, as is the strange connection between Mary Seton and the lawyer who defended Marie Antoinette in 1793. And Talleyrand did visit Maine in 1794.

Mary Clough is fictional. But Captain Stephen Clough and his ship *Sally* were real, and they were in Le Havre during the French Revolution's Reign of Terror, when many royalists were arrested and executed. And a prominent Bostonian, James Swan, who'd fought in the American Revolution with Clough and lived in Paris for several years, was a friend of Lafayette and Talleyrand—and had a financial interest in the *Sally*.

Was Stephen Clough part of one of the attempts to free Queen Marie Antoinette?

We'll probably never know. In the early twentieth century, weary of answering questions about Marie Antoinette, the wife of one of Clough's descendants instructed her grandson to dump all the family's papers and ships' logs into the river. He filled his skiff twice. The papers were lost forever.

I believe Captain Clough, perhaps after failing to free the queen, was trying to help other royalist friends of James Swan's to escape from France. They filled his ship with their belongings in preparation for their journey, but were seized and executed before they could sail.

About forty thousand people were arrested and guillotined during the Reign of Terror that began in 1793.

Captain Clough left Le Havre and sailed to Boston, where James Swan's family claimed his ship's contents.

Today a room at the Museum of Fine Arts in Boston is filled with eighteenth- and early nineteenth-century French furnishings from James Swan's estate. His portrait, painted by John Singleton Copley (1738–1815), looks over furniture and porcelains and tapestries, some of which may have come from Captain Clough's ship, *Sally*.

And although there are few, if any, Marys in the Clough family, Captain Stephen Clough named his youngest daughter, born after his most famous voyage, Hannah Antoinette. To this day there's an Antoinette in every generation of his family.

History or legend? You decide.

I know the story well because in the 1950s my family purchased the old Clough home. It's where I live and write today. I often think of the people who lived here in the past. Perhaps their spirits remain. But their ghosts must be content. They don't disturb me.

Thank you to Pamela Parmal and Meredith Montague of the Textile and Fashion Arts division of the Museum of Fine Arts in Boston, and to Kathy Lynn Emerson, author and expert on Elizabethan England, for their help.

If you're interested in learning more about Mary, Queen of Scots', embroidery I suggest consulting Margaret Swain's *The Needlework of Mary Queen of Scots*, Michael Bath's *Emblems For a Queen: The Needlework of Mary Queen of Scots*, Santina M. Levey's *An Elizabethan Inheritance: The Hardwick Hall Textiles*, Lanto Synge's *Antique Needlework,* George Wingfield Digby's *Elizabethan Embroidery,* and the National Trust's *Hardwick Hall*.

Many books are available on the life and times of Queen Mary and her cousin Elizabeth, and of Marie Antoinette.

If you're interested in stitching Elizabethan embroidery patterns, see Dorothy Clarke's *Exploring Elizabethan Embroidery*, which includes a number of designs by Stephanie Powell based on Elizabethan motifs. And if you'd like to know more about the various gadgets and devices used by needlepointers in the past, see Bridget McConnel's *The Story of Antique Needlework Tools*.

I thank the real Cos Curran, whose grandmother, Kate, won a character naming in a benefit for the Wiscasset Library, for the use of her name, and the real Sarah Byrne, who is from Australia, for the use of hers. As always, I thank my caring and patient husband, artist Bob Thomas, for living with a wife immersed in her writing. My sister Nancy Cantwell for being a "first reader." My writing friends, especially Kathy Lynn Emerson, Kate Flora, and Barbara Ross, for their encouragement and support. And thank you to all the readers of *Twisted Threads*, the first in the Mainely Needlepoint series, who reviewed the book, needled me about minor errors (I'm still learning the fascinating craft of needlepoint), and encouraged me to continue Angie's story.

I thank my agent, John Talbot, my editor, John Scognamiglio, and all the hardworking people at Kensington Publishing, especially publicist extraordinaire Morgan Elwell, who brought Angie and Charlotte and the Mainely Needlepointers to so many readers.

As always, any errors in *Thread and Gone* are mine.

I invite you to friend me on Facebook and Goodreads, check my Web site at www.leawait.com for more about me and my books, including discussion questions for groups reading *Thread and Gone*, and read www.MaineCrimeWriters.com, the blog I write with other authors who write mysteries set in the wonderful, and sometimes mysterious, state of Maine.

Lea Wait

Please turn the page for an exciting
sneak peek of the next
Mainely Needlepoint Mystery

DANGLING BY A THREAD

coming in November 2016!

Chapter 1

"Time has wings and swiftly flies
Youth and Beauty Fade away
Virtue is the only Prize
Whose Joys never will decay."

—Sampler stitched by Chloe Trask in
   Middlesex County, Massachusetts,
   about 1800. Originally dated with four
   digits, in later years someone (probably
   Chloe herself) removed the stitching
   on the final two numbers to conceal
   her age.

The August fog was damp and soft on my face.
I sat on a bench on Wharf Street, watched an-
chored boats in Haven Harbor appear and
disappear in the mists, and sipped my coffee.

A man in a small gray skiff rowed smoothly
toward shore, out of the morning fog. Whoever
he was, he knew the waters and was at home with

them. I watched as he tied his skiff to the town pier and pulled himself onto the dock. That's when I realized something was wrong with his left leg.

I knew Haven Harbor's boats and their owners. I didn't remember ever seeing that skiff or its occupant.

I'd been back in Haven Harbor over three months now, and was beginning to feel comfortable again in the house that had seen both the joys and pains of my growing up. I'd agreed to stay six months; settle in, manage Mainely Needlepoint, the business Gram had started, and come to terms with the past.

I was already thinking six months wasn't long enough. I'd be staying longer.

Still, some mornings, like today, I was restless.

When I felt like that nothing but the sights and sounds of the sea would soothe me. Those ten years I'd spent in Arizona, far from the consistent tides I'd depended on to bring order to my life, had left a hole that only closeness to the water could fill.

Too often in the past weeks I'd woken to the motors of lobster boats leaving the docks and the screeching of the gulls who followed them.

I'd fill a travel mug with coffee and head for the wharves, where I could be close to the sea; could smell the salt air and dried rockweed.

This morning heavy gray fog covered the harbor, hiding the three islands that protected it from the ocean's strength. In the distance I heard the motor of a lobster boat making early morning stops to check traps just outside the harbor.

The man tied his skiff to the end of the town pier. He was tall and thin, with skin almost the color of his straggly gray beard. He might have been forty, or sixty. His flannel shirt hung on him as though it was intended for someone heavier; someone stronger. His jeans were tied with a rope.

He walked up the ramp toward where I was sitting, limping, but not hesitating. Not looking at me or at Arvin Fraser, who'd finished hoisting his bait barrels on board the *Little Lady* and was preparing to leave the dock with Rob Trask, his sternman.

Whoever that man was, he was on a mission.

Curious, I watched him head south on Wharf Street until his figure was lost in the fog.

I walked down the ramp to where Arvin and Rob were preparing to cast off.

"Morning Angie," said Rob. "You're out early again."

"Who was that man?" I asked. I pointed to his skiff, gray as the morning, "The man who rowed in."

Arvin grinned. "Guess you ain't never seen him before. He's a character, but he don't bother no one. Lives out on one of the islands beyond the Three Sisters."

"I didn't know anyone lived out there," I said. "Islands there are just outcroppings of ledges. No houses that I remember. No water, no electricity. Just birds."

"Right," said Rob. "He don't seem to mind, though. Been out there a couple of years."

"What's his name?" I asked.

Arvin and Rob looked at each other. Arvin shrugged. "Don't rightly know. Folks in town call him The Solitary."

Books by Lea Wait

Mainely Needlepoint Mystery Series
Twisted Threads (#1)

Threads of Evidence (#2)

Thread and Gone (#3)

Shadows Antique Print Mystery Series
Shadows at the Fair (#1)

Shadows on the Coast of Maine (#2)

Shadows on the Ivy (#3)

Shadows at the Spring Show (#4)

Shadows of a Down East Summer (#5)

Shadows on a Cape Cod Wedding (#6)

Shadows on a Maine Christmas (#7)

Historical Novels for Ages 8 and Up
Stopping to Home

Seaward Born

Wintering Well

Finest Kind

Uncertain Glory

Nonfiction
Living and Writing on the Coast of Maine

Grab These Cozy Mysteries
from
Kensington Books